Bane rushed to the door, barking.

"Down!" Gracie yelled.

Gunshots riddled the cabin, shattering the windows. She and Cameron hid behind the couch as bullets pelted off the walls and furniture.

Gracie crept to the window, searching for the shooter, when the gunfire ceased.

"We're going after him." Gracie snapped on Bane's leash. "Bane, hunt!"

They exited the cabin, and Bane sniffed the path, tugging against the lead. Gracie's senses were on high alert. Her pulse raged in her ears, making it hard to hear any movement. As they entered the forest, she kept Bane's leash short, forcing him to stick close to her.

Suddenly, a blast and bullet pierced the tree trunk beside her. Gracie dived, yanking the K-9 down with her...

* * *

DAKOTA K-9 UNIT

Chasing a Kidnapper by Laura Scott, April 2025
Deadly Badlands Pursuit by Sharee Stover, May 2025
Standing Watch by Terri Reed, June 2025
Cold Case Peril by Maggie K. Black, July 2025
Tracing Killer Evidence by Jodie Bailey, August 2025
Threat of Revenge by Jessica R. Patch, September 2025
Double Protection Duty by Sharon Dunn, October 2025
Final Showdown by Valerie Hansen, November 2025
Christmas K-9 Patrol by Lynette Eason and
Lenora Worth, December 2025

Colorado native **Sharee Stover** lives in the Midwest with her real-life-hero husband, youngest child and her obnoxiously lovable German shepherd. A self-proclaimed word nerd, she loves the power of words to transform, ignite and restore. She writes Christian romantic suspense combining heart-racing, nail-biting suspense and the delight of falling in love all in one. Connect with her at www.shareestover.com.

Books by Sharee Stover

Love Inspired Suspense

Secret Past
Silent Night Suspect
Untraceable Evidence
Grave Christmas Secrets
Cold Case Trail
Tracking Concealed Evidence
Framing the Marshal
Defending the Witness
Seeking Justice
Guarded by the Marshal

Mountain Country K-9 Unit

Her Duty Bound Defender

Dakota K-9 Unit

Deadly Badlands Pursuit

Visit the Author Profile page at LoveInspired.com.

DEADLY BADLANDS PURSUIT

SHAREE STOVER

Special thanks and acknowledgment are given to Sharee Stover for her contribution to the Dakota K-9 Unit miniseries.

ISBN-13: 978-1-335-63868-7

Recycling programs for this product may not exist in your area.

Deadly Badlands Pursuit

For questions and comments about the quality of this book, please contact us at CustomerService@Harlequin.com.

Love Inspired
22 Adelaide St. West, 41st Floor
Toronto, Ontario M5H 4E3, Canada
www.LoveInspired.com

Printed in U.S.A.

The Lord is my rock, and my fortress, and my deliverer; my God, my strength, in whom I will trust; my buckler, and the horn of my salvation, and my high tower.

—*Psalm* 18:2

For my precious granddaughter, Lennox Elaine.
You are loved beyond measure, little one.
May you grow in grace and in the knowledge
of our Lord and Savior, Jesus Christ.
To Him be the glory both now and forever.

ONE

"Where would you prefer to start, Bane? A missing witness or tracing a gun trafficker's connections?" Deputy US Marshal Gracie Fitzpatrick stroked her K-9 partner's velvety head. "Don't answer that, I already know what you'll say."

Her Belgian Malinois panted contentedly beside her. The newer model gray Chevy Silverado—one of the many benefits of her job—was equipped with a built-in canine kennel that consumed half of her back seat. Protective temperature controls ensured the dog's safety while riding or waiting inside the vehicle. The kennel divider permitted Bane to be close to Gracie, as well as sequestering him when necessary. Her unmarked unit, armed with hidden lights and a siren, maintained its official capacity while allowing her to travel inconspicuously. Only the kennel gave away her law-enforcement status, which wasn't always a bad thing.

Except when Gracie and Bane required an incognito presence while hunting down a fugitive—the greatest skill the two of them possessed. Though

Gracie joked Bane was the talent, she just held the leash.

She was excited to put their skills to the test with her latest career move, joining the Dakota Gun Task Force. The team had been commissioned to identify and apprehend a dangerous weapons-trafficking ring operating across North and South Dakota. The team's mission became personal when the traffickers were suspected of killing a Plains City Police Department K-9 detective, Kenyon Graves. Being part of DGTF—an elite group of law-enforcement professionals including deputy US marshals, ATF and FBI agents, as well as law-enforcement canine handlers from North and South Dakota—was a dream come true for Gracie.

Her cell phone rang, and she answered using her Bluetooth. "Fitzpatrick."

"Just checking in," Daniel Slater, ATF Supervisory Special Agent and the DGTF leader, replied.

"I'm about an hour out," Gracie said.

"Do you need any information from us before making contact?"

"Negative. Our POA is as follows," Gracie responded, referencing the plan of action. "Since it's late already, Bane and I will check in at the Pronghorn Hills Guest Ranch and confirm Cameron Holmes's status." That was the first part of her mission—make contact with a man in WITSEC who hadn't checked in with his handler lately. Then, she and Bane would move on to do the task force work they'd been recruited for—finding out more information about a recently deceased gun trafficker named Petey Pawners. "First thing tomorrow, we'll attempt to locate Pawners's relatives near Black Hawk." The team had recently discovered he had family in the small town, and Gracie was conducting the interviews. It was one of the few clues they had in finding out who the traffickers were…and therefore discovering Kenyon's murderers. Gracie had drawn the most-acquainted-with-the-area straw, having grown up nearby.

Gracie accepted the mission as divine appointment, giving her an escape from her personal life and home in Plains City. Nothing like a backstabbing, betraying ex-boyfriend to kick her motivation into gear. She shook off the thought. Rod O'Dell had already stolen too much of her attention and emotions. She wouldn't give him a second more.

"Excellent," Daniel replied, drawing her back to the present conversation.

Bane gave a sharp bark.

Daniel chuckled. "I assume Bane's disgruntled with the arrangement?"

"Well, he had to voice his opinion," Gracie quipped. "As if we're unaware he'd prefer tracking a fugitive through the wilderness. Though that skill will have to be put on hold until we get these weapons traffickers."

"We're grateful to have both of you on this case," Daniel said. "Has your boss heard anything from Silas Rutherford?" He referred to Cameron Holmes's previously assigned handler. The deputy

US marshal had recently retired, and Cameron had gone MIA.

"Negative."

Supervisory Deputy US Marshal Dallas Brafford had advised that Holmes had failed to report in. Gracie had seen witnesses get overly dependent or attached to their handlers, and struggle to transfer to a new one. For all the marshals knew, Cameron was being defiant. Gracie wasn't passing judgment—there could be a lot of reasons for his lack of compliance. Besides, she'd not been assigned to handle witness protection to date. Once she and Bane located Holmes, they'd pass him off to someone with a bigger paycheck.

"I figure it'll be a quick stop," Gracie continued. "The guy probably just lost his cell phone or went fishing and disregarded his annually scheduled check-in. It's not as if he's new to the rules." After witnessing his parents' murder at age eighteen, Holmes was transferred into WITSEC, where he'd lived under protection for the past twelve years. The murderer, Walter Quigley, a once prominent politician, was still serving the last thirteen years of a twenty-five-year prison sentence.

"Let's hope," Daniel said. "Please update the team after you've conducted the interviews."

"Roger that."

They disconnected.

Since the death of her parents and sister five years prior, Gracie had avoided this part of the state because of the accompanying memories that assailed her. At times, the intensity of the past confined her in a restrictive hold, hindering her ability to breathe. For the purposes of this trip, she'd only have to endure Black Hawk for the interviews. She'd shift her brain into marshal mode long enough to complete the task. She snorted—at the rate she racked up painful relationship memories, she was running out of towns in South Dakota to avoid.

Bane nudged her arm as though sensing her emotional shift…or maybe he just wanted out of the kennel. "Tell you what, buddy, once we've confirmed Mr. Holmes is alive and well, I'll take you for a long run," she said.

He retreated into his section, clearly satisfied.

"C'mon, look at this," Gracie said encouragingly, focusing her attention on the gorgeous landscape of Badlands National Park that surrounded them. She inhaled fresh air through the open window.

Broken sections of green grass and soil, called sod tables, had sprouted amid the multicolored layered formations of various stones, volcanic ash and shale. As she traveled along Badlands Loop Scenic Byway, she marveled at the unbroken prairie that stretched north, taking her closer to Cameron Holmes's property, the Pronghorn Hills Guest Ranch. Gracie rolled down her window. Night had descended, and the sweet scents of South Dakota's late spring carried in the cool May breeze that filtered through the truck cab.

The landscape triggered Gracie's memories, reminding her of the many family trips she'd taken growing up here. Her father had loved geography and found opportunities to insert teachable moments in everyday life. She recalled his words about God's natural processes creating the beauty they appreciated in the Badlands. The two main ones were called deposition and erosion. Deposition stacked layers of matter that created the artistic lines within the formations, while erosion stripped away the rock and stone, tearing it apart to create the varying degrees.

Just like Gracie's heart.

The trauma she had endured after losing her parents and baby sister in the horrible airplane crash had trapped her in a vise of pain. At times, she hadn't known whether she'd survive. After the atrocities she and Leigh endured thanks to accidentally seeing a murder, Gracie had thought her family's troubles were behind her. Apparently, she'd been wrong. But then Rod O'Dell entered her life shortly thereafter. For the first time, Gracie had experienced falling in love. If only she'd known then what loving him would cost her. The deposition of his acidic love was stripped bare by the erosion of betrayal in the worst kind.

Yet God continually cared for her. Her career with the marshals and getting recruited for DGTF had positively rebuilt those missing places. Perhaps that was what life was all about. Stripping away and reconstructing. Though in Gracie's case, it seemed the erosion was happening at a much faster rate.

The varying sod tables soaked up rain during intense storms. Though the exposed rock around them also wore away, it happened at a slower rate. Maybe it was all about perspective. The tables weren't protection from the deterioration, they were a product of it. Inevitably, both faced the same fate.

"I'm in my head too much," Gracie said aloud, shifting her philosophical pondering to the allegedly missing witness.

Cameron Holmes had purchased the guest ranch two years prior. It was no big stretch for Gracie's mind as to why he would do so. South Dakota offered rich landscape and incredible atmosphere. A guest ranch most likely provided a profitable income while permitting Cameron to relax.

More certain than ever that the witness was fine, Gracie looked forward to enjoying the rest of the evening in her cabin.

An hour later, she pulled up to the property entrance. Her headlights bounced off the closed black iron gates, where a small scone light illuminated the keypad. Gracie shifted into Park and withdrew her phone with the details regarding her scheduled stay. For all Cameron or his personnel knew, Gracie and Bane were visiting the grounds as tourists.

She was wearing dark cargo pants and a black long-sleeved shirt. Nothing about her appearance, except her leg holster and Glock, revealed that she was law enforcement, which gave her exactly what she needed to approach unsuspecting fugitives. Though Cameron didn't fit that bill, she didn't want to alert anyone about her identity. Gracie didn't necessarily expect the gun traffickers to be in the area, however, they were dangerous, and the team was certain the group was spread throughout the Dakotas.

She scrolled through her email to the welcome message that included the gate code. It also warned the number would change regularly to ensure privacy and prohibit unscheduled visitors to the grounds. Gracie doubted Cameron followed through with the recoding. More than likely, it was used to advise visitors they couldn't come onto the property on a whim.

The message advised her to check in at the main ranch house and pick up her key and welcome basket, along with the details of her cabin rental.

Bane hopped up from his position in the kennel and poked his head through the divider.

"Wait here," she ordered, sliding out of the driver's seat. She shut the door with Bane watching her protectively. She chuckled at his intense stare as she moved to the gate's coded keypad. Gracie entered the number, which elicited three beeps and a green light, indicating success in unlocking the gate.

She rushed into the driver's seat as the iron doors slowly swung open, then drove down the long, winding lane through the towering pine trees. The atmosphere was bathed in the intoxicating aroma of pine, and the moonlight cast shadows across the cabins.

"Wow," Gracie breathed.

When she reached the main ranch house, which

resembled luxe cabins she'd seen in magazines, she parked in the space designated *Guest* by the posted sign. "Okay, Bane, stay here until I get the cabin key." She considered her Glock in the console beside her. She never went anywhere without the weapon, or Bane, for that matter, but she didn't want to draw attention to herself. She decided to tuck the gun behind her back, concealing it with her shirt, and opted to leave Bane secured in the vehicle.

The Malinois snorted his displeasure and pinned her with a look that had her second-guessing her options.

"Don't pout. I'll only be gone a second," she assured him.

She exited the truck, locked the doors and approached a set of steps on the wooden porch positioned on the side. A bright neon sign hung on the door and read *Office*.

Crickets chirped from their hidden places amid the bushes that lined the walkway. Gracie made a spontaneous decision to extend her stay and commute to Black Hawk for the interviews.

Gracie raised her hand to ring the bell when a beefy hand clamped over her mouth, tugging her backward in a powerful hold. The sound of a gun cocking against her ear froze her in place.

"Perfect bait," the raspy male voice said. He reached past her and pounded on the door. "Come on out, James Dunwood," he called in a singsong voice.

Gracie inwardly gasped. James Dunwood was Cameron's *old name*—the one he had for eighteen years before obtaining his witness-protection identity.

"Or your girlfriend dies," the thug added.

Gracie struggled against the attacker, but his cement-tight grip made movement nearly impossible. Mentally berating herself for leaving Bane in the truck, she reassessed. The reflection in the door's small window revealed her attacker was wearing a black ski mask. Of course, the prime clothing choice for felons. He peered past her, focused on the door, clearly distracted by the expectation of Cameron's response. She anticipated he'd shove her forward to throw off Cameron and overtake him.

Not on her watch.

"James!" the man bellowed.

Gracie took the advantage, and thrust her boot into the man's knee, hyperextending the joint. The practiced move worked perfectly. Her attacker grunted loudly, stumbling back on his good leg, and momentarily loosened his grip on her.

Something—just a blur in her peripheral vision—barreled into the assailant.

His gun flew over the handrail and clattered onto the stone path.

Gracie bolted off the porch in one leap and scurried to the side of the cabin for cover.

She instantly recognized the tall, dark-haired interference. Cameron Holmes.

The two men engaged in hand-to-hand combat, giving Gracie the diversion she needed.

She inched closer and ducked behind a flowering bush. She withdrew her gun and aimed for the attacker's head. But the men battled, constantly shifting positions and obstructing a clear shot.

Over Cameron's shoulder, the masked man spotted Gracie's gun and shoved Cameron toward her before lobbing a small statue in her direction. He lunged off the porch and disappeared around the corner.

Gracie gave chase, but the man seemed to vanish, fleeing south toward Badlands National Park.

Cameron spun to face her.

"Stay here. I need my dog!" Gracie didn't wait for his response and sprinted for the pickup to release Bane.

The dog hopped down, eager to roll.

"Zook!" She used the German command for *find* and kneeled, allowing Bane to catch of whiff of the attacker's scent from her shirt before repeating the command, "Bane, *Zook*!"

The Malinois sprinted south into the thick copse of trees and foliage. Gracie bolted after him, and Cameron's heavy footfalls thudded behind her.

"Go back!" Gracie called over her shoulder, not slowing down. She wouldn't let the perp get away.

In the distance, Bane's sharp barks erupted through the forest, getting her attention.

Gracie shifted direction, racing toward the sound.

Cameron Holmes kept pace with the woman until she skidded to a halt, and he nearly collided with her. She stared in disbelief at the vacant dirt road that bordered the edge of the park beyond his property. The growl of an engine and a cloud of dust fading in the distance indicated they were too late. The dog, a Belgian Malinois if he was correct in the breed description, whined and circled the tire tracks that testified to the assailant's earlier presence.

His chest ached from the exertion of the run, and he gasped, catching his breath. After days of enduring suspicion and fear, he'd finally come face-to-face with the attacker. And he'd escaped. Conflicting emotions warred within Cameron, teetering between curiosity at the woman's identity and disappointment the attacker had gotten away.

"Bane had him," the woman grumbled, drawing Cameron's attention.

At the mention of his name, the dog returned to her side.

Cameron studied the duo. "Can't deny I'm impressed at his ability to track the man through the forest."

She was wearing cargo pants, boots and a dark T-shirt. Nothing revealed her identity, which she'd not yet provided for him.

"Super disappointed he didn't just attack the guy," Cameron confessed.

"Unfortunately, it doesn't work like that." One corner of the woman's lip quirked upward.

"Is that what *zook* means?"

"No. We use German commands rather than English ones in K-9 training so civilians don't try tossing out unsolicited orders to our dogs. *Zook* means find." She withdrew a leash from her pocket. "Bane, come." The Malinois immediately sat, and she snapped on the lead, then faced Cameron. "Which way would he go? Where's this road go?"

Cameron felt the dog's stare on him, but he knew better than to return the gesture. He'd not antagonize the muscular creature. "Depends."

"On?"

"This isn't some major bypass. You're on the outskirts of the Badlands National Park. That road curves and splits beyond the bend, spreading out to several other less-traveled paths in varying directions." Cameron gestured wide with his arms. "And since we don't have a clue what he drove, especially in regard to four-wheel-drive capability, which would only further complicate the possibilities, it all just—"

"Depends," she said, finishing his thought. "Fantastic. Well, it's apparent he's fine with killing people, so I surmise four-wheeling off road where it's not permitted wouldn't be entirely out of the question."

Cameron grinned despite the seriousness of the situation. He liked her moxie, but he needed information about this stranger before he'd let down his guard. "Who are you?" He'd not intended to be so blunt, but there wasn't time for niceties. Based on her narrowed gaze, he might have to reconsider revising his tactics and deploy a little more finesse. Cameron exhaled and started again. "You handled yourself well back there, and you don't appear shaken after what we just encountered. Your dog seems to have excellent tracking skills." He gestured to the animal, still piercing him with a pointed stare. "I'm guessing you're not just a guest at my ranch?"

"Technically, I am," she replied. "Deputy US Marshal Gracie Fitzpatrick and this is K-9 Bane."

Cameron bit his lip. He'd met plenty of marshals over the years, all mature older men, and she didn't fit the bill. His last handler could've passed for his dad...had his father lived to be that old. Cameron swallowed down the unexpected emotion rising in his throat. He'd never once been contacted by anyone who looked like her.

She withdrew her credentials from the pocket of her cargo pants and passed him the leather pouch, unmoved by his disbelieving stare.

Cameron reviewed the badge and identification card, confirming the petite woman with dark hair and shocking green eyes was, in fact, who she claimed to be. He passed her back the credentials. "Nice to meet you, Ms. Fitzpatrick."

"Deputy Marshal Fitzpatrick," she corrected, pocketing the credentials. "Mr. Holmes, I'm curious as to why you haven't responded to our office's many attempts to reach you? Witness protection is a serious assignment and not open to your whims of communication at your convenience."

Cameron gaped at her admonishment. Indignation overrode his surprise. "Deputy Marshal, your presence here and that—" he searched for the right words "—confrontation we barely survived is *exactly* why I haven't responded to your office."

"If you had reservations or issues, why didn't you reach out for help?" She glanced out at the vacant road as though it provided the answer she sought.

"That's complicated."

She faced him, waiting.

Cameron sighed. "Ever feel like someone's watching you?"

"Ye-e-a-ah—" She dragged out the word for several syllables.

"That's been a constant for me the past few days. Nobody else besides the marshals is aware I'm here."

"Whoa. Hold up." She blinked a few times. "You're not suggesting that another law-enforcement official is responsible for that attack, are you?"

"Absolutely." Cameron spun on his heel and headed back toward the ranch. "It's no coincidence you showed up here at the same time that thug tried killing me. He either followed you..." He didn't finish the insinuation.

"No way." She caught up to him, the dog between them. "Mr. Holmes, two things. Firstly, if I'd planned to kill you, I would've succeeded."

Her comment got his attention.

"And secondly," she continued, "consider why I would lead then fend off an attacker if I meant your demise."

"Duly noted." Cameron couldn't argue her point. "Until today, I had no proof to validate my suspicions. However, if you're not the leak, I'm tasked with worrying about protecting you, too."

Deputy Marshal Fitzgerald's guffaw had Cameron stopping in his tracks. He turned. "Nothing about this situation is humorous to me."

She snorted, waving him off. "No, but your comment was. I believe I've more than proven I don't need your protection. And as I recall, I'm the one with the badge and a gun here."

Cameron commenced walking. "That might be true, but there's more to survival than possession of a firearm and authority to use it."

"Not sure whether I'm offended or intrigued by your comment."

He paused, contemplating what to share. "WITSEC has helped me to stay alive, but it hasn't been the only reason. Criminals come in a variety of social statuses and occupations. I've seen enough not to lay all my survival eggs in one WITSEC shaped basket. Common sense and instincts play a huge part in my life."

"I'm intrigued." She tilted her head, as though considering his words.

He didn't reply. That was more than enough information to share with this stranger...for now. Thankfully, she didn't press.

The chirping of birds overhead resumed, reminding Cameron why he'd chosen this place to build and settle down. Two years of serenity and peace had suddenly become a place where he feared danger behind every tree and bush. He'd come down hard on the marshal and needed to find neutral ground. "Your dog is amazing."

The defensiveness in her posture fizzled out. "Bane is an experienced tracker—as you witnessed—and he's got protection skills."

Had she included that detail as a warning for him? The dog shifted in place, walking between him and the marshal, as though emphasizing the words.

"Yeah." Cameron chuckled. "I gathered that, as well." The smile she shot at him tore through his reserves. "Hey, Deputy Marshal Fitzgerald, I need to apologize. I shouldn't have snapped at you like that. I'm stressed with danger worries. Now after that thug called me by name, I can't help but wonder if the past has returned to finish me off years after my parents' murder. I'm a little on edge and not myself."

"Understandable. You've spent twelve years in Witness Protection, why now?" she asked.

"I'm sure you're aware of my history."

"WITSEC isn't my specialty. My knowledge is limited to what's in your file."

He pushed back the low-hanging tree branches and held them so they could both pass. "Walter Quigley, my parents' murderer, is safely behind bars." He paused. "Unless you've got other information?"

"Nope," she said. "That's accurate. Quigley's still incarcerated."

Cameron continued walking. "So what's changed?"

"I wish I could tell you."

They stepped out of the foliage and entered the clearing on the edge of his property. "With Silas Rutherford's retirement, are you my new assigned handler?" A part of Cameron hoped she said yes.

"No, that's not my role or responsibility here. I'm part of the Dakota Gun Task Force."

"I'm confused." Cameron led the way to the office. "Why would a task force hunting for gun traffickers want anything to do with me?"

"They don't."

Cameron unlocked the door, holding it open for her and the dog to enter. The small space held two metal desks, a tall metal file cabinet and a laptop Cameron used for the business.

She paused, surveying the office. "Do you run this place by yourself?"

"Yes and no. I have employees to help with the daily duties."

"How many?" She closed the door behind them.

"Three. They're all on vacation right now." He had enough to worry about without fearing his men would be harmed because of the target on his back. Though he'd not witnessed direct attacks yet, the threat was enough. And the few "accidents" around the ranch along with tonight's attack proved he'd not been wrong.

"To address your question regarding the task force, DGTF is comprised of ATF and FBI agents, deputy US marshals and canine handlers from various jurisdictions. When you failed to respond to your scheduled reporting times, my home office requested I conduct a welfare check on you as part of my regular duties."

"Gotcha. Basically, a drive-by." Cameron dropped onto his office chair. "I can't offer any information on weapons trafficking and as you can see, I'm alive." He leaned back, crossing his arms over his chest. "All I did to land a life in WITSEC was to show up at the wrong place at the wrong time." Liar. A better son would've reacted faster and protected his parents.

Oblivious to his silent contemplations, Fitzgerald dropped onto a chair opposite him, Bane beside her. "I'll notify the powers that be that you're alive and in danger. Your new handler will be in touch with you. Please make every effort to respond to his or her messages."

"Point taken, but negative," he replied. "Notify the marshals that until I feel safe, I'm not replying to anyone." She opened her mouth to speak, and he blurted, "Deputy Marshal, no offense, but I counted on your office to protect me. It's clear by today's attack, they're unable to handle that responsibility."

"I empathize with you." Her expression softened. "Please call me Gracie."

Cameron took the offer as an olive branch of

peace between them. "Nice to meet you, Gracie." He leaned across the desk and shook her hand. "Cameron Holmes. At least I have been for the last decade."

"I must admit, when that thug called you James Dunwood, it surprised me."

"You're telling me." Cameron sat back. "I haven't heard my real name for so long I had almost forgotten it."

One corner of her mouth quirked upward.

"Sorry, I have a dry sense of humor."

"No apologies. I understand living this way can't be easy on you."

"Water under the witness bridge," he replied. "I need to figure out how to proceed."

"I'd start with the fact that you're not safe staying here."

Cameron shook his head. "I'm not leaving my ranch. Not until it's the only option left."

"What'd you have in mind?"

He paused. Nobody in the marshals in the past decade had asked Cameron for his opinion on anything. He appreciated the gesture. "There's a security firm I've hired before. I'll request guards to secure the grounds. I've got too much invested here to leave it unattended." He lifted his cell phone. "No offense to you or your capabilities."

She tilted her head, tipping her chin. "Okay."

Cameron dialed the number on speakerphone, allowing Gracie to hear the conversation. He spoke to John at Big Dakotas Security briefly, ensuring he didn't give too much away about his current situation, and was disappointed when the man said he didn't have the capacity to take the job. Cameron disconnected. "Now what?"

Gracie leaned forward. "I think between the three of us, we'll be all right."

Cameron looked around. "There's another marshal coming?"

"No." She stroked the dog's head. "Bane will provide guard duty. However, we cannot be responsible for other guests."

"Actually, besides you, there are no others. I canceled all my bookings to renovate the cabins."

"And because you feared something nefarious was lurking?" she asked.

"Exactly."

She quirked an eyebrow. "And the cabins are under construction?"

"Don't worry. Yours is the only one that's complete. I needed the extra time to finish the rest."

"What about your employees?"

"Without paying guests I can't afford to have them working on other nonpaying projects."

"And you're worried for their safety," Gracie added.

"Precisely. They believe they're getting an extended vacation." He shrugged. "I didn't tell them otherwise."

"Smart."

Cameron studied Gracie, recalling she wasn't

his handler. "I appreciate your offer to help me, but aren't you just passing through?"

"Well, as I explained, I was sent here by my home office as part of my normal duties. I'd say things have changed thanks to that attack. However, before I commit, I'll have to connect with my team." Gracie shifted to sit with one leg tucked under her knee. "I started out on a double mission. It might take a little longer than anticipated."

Cameron smiled and contemplated the task force she mentioned. Surely, it had nothing to do with him, but he was fact-gathering. "Are you allowed to tell me about this gun-trafficking thing?"

"Some. I need to conduct interviews of family and associates of a known murdered trafficker."

Relief coursed through Cameron that Gracie would remain with him for the time being. Except if she was tracking another set of criminals, did having her on his property add to his risk?

What other options did he have?

"Go ahead," Gracie said.

Cameron blinked. "Come again?"

"You're clearly processing something. Spit it out and let's see if we can tackle it together."

Together. When was the last time he'd had anyone offer to help him? Not that he'd have the option of authentic friendships or a romantic relationship while living in WITSEC. His entire life was a lie, a ruse, created to keep him alive. How could he put that another person? Touched, Cameron's worry for her interrupted the appreciation. "I'd love to say everything will be fine, but I can't," he confessed. "I'm on someone's death list, and I don't even know why. Truthfully, I'm concerned they'll use you as bait to lure me out and kill me. Which means they won't leave any witnesses alive." Cameron knew that risk better than anyone.

TWO

"I've encountered some of the worst people you can imagine," Gracie blurted. And why would that be a comfort to Cameron? She inwardly cringed. She'd said it as affirmation of her and Bane's skills. Although before she jumped in hook, line and K-9, she needed to notify the team of the situation. "Just to clarify, you said you've felt endangered for a while?"

"Looking over your shoulder comes with WIT-SEC territory, but lately..." Cameron paused. "I can't offer any evidence beyond a feeling and a few mishaps around the ranch."

"What kind of mishaps?" Gracie studied the handsome man. He was tall and fit, with dark hair and blue eyes. "Don't discount intuition. After all, the attacker called you by your real name."

"Things like my truck's brakes going out and an electrical short to one cabin." Cameron grew quiet, averting his gaze. "Being called James is weird. It's a life and a person I left behind. I barely remember what that part of me was like. I lost everyone who mattered to me. My future was stolen, my family killed and the ranch where I'd grown up was sold out from under me."

Gracie tried recalling the details from the file and couldn't remember that piece. "Where was this?"

"Wyoming. It was in my family for over four generations." Cameron fidgeted with a pen on the desk. "Those things are gone. And you know what? To this day, I still don't understand why." His eyes met hers, and in their depths, Gracie saw the undeniable pain.

"I didn't know," Gracie admitted. The black-and-white facts on a sheet of paper weren't the same as the heart and soul of a wounded survivor.

"Wasn't it enough that Walter Quigley destroyed my life once?" Cameron shoved back from the desk and got to his feet, then began pacing around the office. "Am I going to have to deal with it all over again?"

Compassion for him filled Gracie's heart. "That would be the million-dollar question," she replied softly. "Together, we'll figure this out." *Stop that.* She had no right to commit to his detail without first clearing it. Yet, she wanted to help the guy.

He shot her a disbelieving glance, adding to her contemplations.

"I realize you're concerned there's a leak in the system, so I won't ask you to rely on it." Gracie maintained eye contact. "However, I'd request you to trust me."

Cameron gave a disheartened grunt and said, deadpan, "I suppose that's the only option I have."

"I'm touched by your deep vote of confidence in me," she teased.

His sideways smile made Gracie's stomach flutter. What was wrong with her? "I'll be back. I should make a call."

She pushed away from the desk and walked outside with Bane. Gracie needed a little distance. She'd been around her share of witnesses in the past, though she'd never signed up to be a handler. That wasn't in her repertoire. She and Bane specialized in hunting fugitives, escaped convicts, potential criminals—they thrived on the hunt.

That was until talking to Cameron. She understood his pain on a level others might not. She'd lost everyone who mattered to her, as well. Being an orphan, regardless of the age, wasn't for the weak. Years didn't lessen the impact. Though a horrible accident with no rhyme or reason had stolen Gracie's family, Cameron had lost his parents to a senseless act of cruelty. Not just them, but their family ranch and the inheritance of his future he'd probably planned for since childhood.

She glanced around the beautiful grounds of Pronghorn Guest Ranch. Of course, Cameron excelled here using the skills he'd learned as a kid. He'd surrendered his future for survival. Thrust into WITSEC, where he lived a nonexistent life, basically invisible and without connection. The loneliness had to be consuming. She could contact her boss and request he assign someone else to be Cameron's interim handler.

Contrary to her normal modus operandi, something within Gracie wanted to stay and help him. Yet, she and Bane had proven their capabilities. Working for the elite DGTF was a dream come true. In the meantime, if her boss ordered her to protect Cameron, she'd comply. She enjoyed working with DGTF, however, she was, first and foremost, a deputy US marshal.

Bane whined, regaining her attention.

"You're right, buddy, I don't issue the assignments. Let's make that call." She walked down the porch steps to her vehicle and leaned against the bumper. "Bane, guard." He assumed the position protectively in front of her, attentive to their surroundings.

Gracie withdrew her cell phone and started to dial her boss, Supervisory Deputy US Marshal Dallas Brafford. She paused. Cameron believed someone within the agency was responsible for the leak. Should she wait?

She called the team supervisor at the DGTF instead. "Hey, Daniel," she said when he answered.

"Do you have an update?"

"Yeah, and you're not going to like it." Gracie provided an explanation of the events, ending with Cameron's failed attempt to contract a private security agency.

"Notify your boss. Your first responsibility is to the marshals. We want to maintain our cooperative efforts with them, and I understand your priority to remain there," Daniel stated.

Gracie's heart sank. He was about to tell her they'd replace her on the task force.

"I'll assign Deputy Zach Kelcey to assist with the interviews of Petey Pawners's family and associates. We don't want to lose momentum on that lead."

Had she heard Daniel correctly?

"Gracie?"

"Yes. Agreed." Gracie exhaled a sigh of relief. "Thank you."

"As much as we'd like to handle things in sequential order without overlapping, that's just not how real life works, right?"

Recalling Daniel's most recent interruption in the form of a toddler, Gracie shifted gears.

"How is little Joy?" she asked. She spotted Cameron approaching her from his office and waved him forward. Joy had appeared a month prior, sitting abandoned outside the Plains City PD and ATF shared building with only a redacted copy of a birth certificate and a note claiming her family relationship to Daniel.

"She's a sweet little girl," he said.

"Are there any updates on locating her parents or legal guardians?"

"Not yet. I have taken in Joy…with the approval of Child Protection Services," he quickly added. "And my grandmother is doting on her."

"Aw, I'm sure she's already in love with the child," Gracie replied.

Daniel chuckled. "Yeah, Joy's won her heart."

Gracie paused, curious, but careful to not overstep her boundaries. As though anticipating her question, Daniel said, "I submitted DNA for a familial match test, but the backlog is horrendous. Might be a few weeks before I hear anything."

Relieved, Gracie replied, "It's wise to do that." What would he do if the results were unfavorable? She dared not ask. It wasn't her business.

"With the changes in technology advancements, I hope the results will narrow down the parental possibilities, too. I can't imagine how she's related to me." Weariness hung in his tone.

"Did the birth certificate provide any leads?" Gracie perched on the edge of her truck bumper.

"Still waiting on that, too. I visited the hospital, but there's a system issue."

"Figures..."

Cameron gestured toward Bane, requesting to pet him. Gracie nodded and stretched out her hand, assuring the K-9 it was okay.

"Yeah," Daniel said. "They promised to get back to me ASAP."

"Ugh. Two steps forward."

"One step back," Daniel finished. "I couldn't leave Joy in CPS custody while we're sorting this out. The poor little girl doesn't understand what's happening." He grunted. "Who am I kidding? Neither do I."

Cameron kneeled and scratched Bane's ears, earning him an approving tail thump. Gracie smiled at the two, happily surprised at her dog's fondness of Cameron. "You're taking all the right steps. I'll keep praying. God is in control."

A strange look passed over Cameron's face and he mouthed, *Be right back* before he hurried to his office. What was that about?

"I appreciate your prayers more than you know," Daniel said, interrupting her thoughts. "If Joy is related to me, how? What family members are out there that I've never met? I'm baffled."

"It's a lot to process." What Gracie would give to learn she had family and wasn't alone in the world.

"Thanks, Gracie. I'll notify Zach. Keep me updated."

"Will do."

They disconnected, then Gracie pushed off from the truck bumper and withdrew a flashlight from the console. A text vibrated and she checked the screen. It was from Daniel:

Zach will arrive by 0800 tomorrow.

Wow, that was fast. Gracie typed Roger that, then pocketed the phone. At least she'd have reinforcements.

She rounded the rear of the pickup, scanning the area. Only the sounds of crickets chirruping invaded the serenity of the moment. Based on the little she'd seen of the property, there was a lot of ground to cover. Bane was brilliant and skilled, but he was a single resource. If they were to keep Cameron safe, they needed help.

"C'mon, Bane." The dog quickly moved to her side, and they walked to the office. She rapped twice on the door before entering.

"Come in," Cameron called.

Gracie and Bane stepped inside.

Cameron sat behind his desk. "I apologize for interrupting your call. It seemed personal."

She noticed the clipped tone. Had something offended him? "No, I was talking to my task force leader."

Skepticism creased his forehead. "About praying?"

Hmm, so that was it. "Yes."

He averted his gaze. "Were you able to work out a plan for me?"

"Yes, he is sending another deputy by morning," she said.

"Great. More cops?"

"Just one. I didn't express your concerns…yet." She added the last part to remind him where her loyalties lie.

Cameron frowned, but to his credit, he didn't complain.

Realigning the discussion, she said, "I'd like to recon the property."

"Sure." Cameron rose, leading the way out, and locked the door behind them. "I'll check on my horses."

Surprised, Gracie increased her pace. "Where are they?" In the darkness, it was hard to see the full extent of the land.

"They're secure in the stables."

"Let's start there." They moved together in silence, Gracie visually surveying the landscape.

Massive boulders dotted the area amid a variety of blooming trees laden with leaves. Pine trees stood in Christmas-tree-perfect condition along the road that led to the cabins. The rugged South Dakota mountains surrounded them in varying shades, though the darkness veiled the details. Cameron directed her to a large stable. He entered a code in the keypad, then released the lock and held open the door.

"I can't wait to see this place in the daylight," she said.

An automated light overhead illuminated the spotless space. Gracie's attention turned to the stalls, where two beautiful horses stood, watching.

"Two years here has given me that false sense of sanctuary. Tonight was a reality check." Cameron moved to the first one. "Hey, Rocket." He reached in, gently stroking the horse's muzzle.

"What's this one's name?" Gracie stepped closer.

"Sugar."

She turned to see an almost identical horse standing at the gate. "Is it okay to pet her?"

"Absolutely."

Gracie reached in and touched the horse's velvety nose. "Hello, there." Bane sniffed the floor, intrigued with the new smells.

Once Cameron was certain the horses were safe, they exited the stables, and he led Gracie around the property.

Four guest cabins were situated in a circular pattern and spaced apart, allowing privacy while maintaining the appearance of a small community. "I'll clear them," Gracie said, withdrawing her gun.

Cameron opened the first door, and they moved through each of the quaint cabins. Construction equipment and tools littered the interiors, evidence of Cameron's renovation claims. Lastly, he showed Gracie to her assigned cabin—the only one that didn't bear proof of an in-progress status. Farthest from the others, she was pleasantly surprised at the accommodations. "I'll grab my things once we've completed the reconnaissance." He handed her the keys, and she pocketed them.

Satisfied the perpetrator wasn't lurking in one of the units, they circled the full length of the grounds, then returned to Cameron's cabin.

"How long will the repairs take?" she asked.

"They're mainly cosmetic. There's no lack of competition in hospitality for customers. I want to remain competitive."

"I don't have a lot of experience when it comes to guest ranches, but I'd say this place is ideal for anyone wanting to get away," Gracie said. "I'm glad Zach will be here to help provide protection detail."

Cameron faced her. "How well do you know this guy?"

"We've worked together awhile. He's a deputy sheriff in Keystone." Gracie stood, prepared to end the discussion. Aware she'd not provided Cameron with the reassurance he wanted, she replied, "I trust him, if that's what you're asking."

"It is." Cameron sighed. "If you say he's good, I'll have to take your word."

Bane rushed ahead, pausing near a boulder.

"What's up, Bane?"

The Malinois fixated his gaze at the darkness, emitting a low warning growl. Cameron whirled around, searching for the source. Gracie withdrew her gun and moved in front of him.

The silence was deafening. Even the crickets had stopped chirping. Gracie lifted her hand, advising Cameron to remain quiet. She watched Bane for any indication of what potential danger he'd homed in on. But the dog remained stoic.

Gracie crept forward, scanning the darkness.

Bane stayed beside her, Cameron trailing. Seeing nothing, she started to lower her gun.

A blast from behind sent the group diving for cover within a grove of trees that bordered the property. "Stay down," Gracie ordered Cameron and Bane simultaneously.

They were at the farthest side of the property and since they'd walked, her vehicle and the shelter of the cabins and main office were out of reach. They couldn't run in that direction without compromising their position and exposing themselves to the shooter.

Had the assailant circled back and waited for this opportunity? A chill ran down Gracie's spine at the possibility. How had she been so foolish?

Gracie peered around the tree trunk in the direction where the first shots had come from. Everything went silent.

Had the shooter fled?

In reply to her unspoken question, the air erupted again in a second round of gunfire.

Cameron stayed low as shards of the massive boulder flicked him while Gracie returned fire.

Bane remained close, panting. Though Cameron was no expert on animal behavior, the gunfire no doubt stressed him out as much as it bothered Cameron.

Frustrated by his lack of weapon to assist, Cameron inched to the side, attempting to gain a better visual of the attacker.

Slivers of rock pricked his cheek, forcing him to duck. "Do you think there's more than one shooter?"

"Or he's using an automatic rifle," Gracie said, twisting to face him. "Somewhere to the south."

Exactly what Cameron feared. Where the thick evergreen tree line bordered the property and added to the wilderness appeal of his cabins. Simultaneously, it provided ample hiding places for the attacker. Seeking shelter at the cabins meant running straight toward danger.

Not an option.

The gunfire was relentless. One skilled shooter with two automatic weapons or two taking turns? Either way, they were outgunned.

Gracie checked her magazine. "I can't hold him off much longer."

Cameron gazed out to the vast wilderness of Badlands National Park behind them. The uneven landscape rose and fell, creating a jagged horizon. If they reached the stone formations, they'd have sufficient shelter. However, doing so required the trio to run out into the open, fully exposed to the bullets.

The gunfire drew closer. "He's closing in on us," Gracie said.

"We have to make a run for it out there."

"How?"

"You want me to trust you, right?"

She gave a slight nod, confusion in her expression.

"Then I'm asking you to do the same. I know this land."

Several more shots echoed around them, proclaiming the shooter's intention to drive them out and force them to surrender.

Cameron refused to give in, but he wouldn't leave Gracie behind.

Gracie looked down at her gun. "We can't use the flashlight. How well do you know your way around?" She jerked her chin toward the foliage and multicolored rock formations behind them.

"Very well."

"We've got no other option." Gracie exhaled. "We can't stay here."

"My thoughts exactly."

Gracie slid her gun into her waistband. "Then we have to go now." She snagged Bane's leash. "We'll follow you."

"Stay close."

"Wait for him to reload, then we run," Gracie advised.

The atmosphere grew quiet.

"Now!"

Cameron scurried to his feet, and they sprinted, weaving and ducking around the sod tables and formations before diving behind a layered patch of sand and rock.

The gunfire resumed, keeping up with them.

Cameron surveyed the area, spotting the next goal. "Keep going!" He led Gracie through the sparse land, staying close to the massive rocks. They stumbled over the dry prairie, where grassy clumps littered the uneven ground. To the untrained eye, the randomness of the badlands, with its many rows and multicolored formations, played tricks on the viewer's perception. Cameron hoped it would keep the shooter from tracing them as they moved deeper into the wilderness.

Shots echoed, carried on the wind, disguising the assailant's position.

Only the moon provided a measure of ambient light. The warm afternoon had transitioned into a cooler evening. Shadows splayed across the vast area, providing further concealment. However, it also prevented them from seeing dangerous camouflaged wildlife. Cameron refrained from sharing those details with Gracie. It would only hinder their escape. Hopefully, the gunfire would cause the creatures to scatter.

At last, they reached the buttes and pinnacles that jetted toward the sky, surrounding them like an open-ceiling castle. Hidden between the majestic spires, Cameron had discovered a few small hollows he'd earmarked for a situation like tonight.

Neither spoke as they climbed through the narrow gaps between rocks. Cameron spotted the cave, concealed by low-hanging grasses. "Come on," he whispered, entering first and pausing to scan for wildlife.

Seeing nothing of concern, he waved Gracie and Bane inside and they moved to the side, steering clear of the entrance.

The gunshots became sporadic, fading but still present.

"Maybe he lost us," Gracie said.

"Let's hope. The shadows here should conceal us as long as he doesn't get too close."

"Great," Gracie mumbled.

Footsteps crunched on the hard earth outside. Nearby.

Bane emitted a guttural growl.

Gracie lifted her hand in what Cameron assumed was a command to be quiet. The dog instantly obeyed, but his ears stayed perked, and his gaze fixed on the entrance.

Cameron homed in, trying to distinguish whether there was more than one attacker. "Not sure if it's one or two," he whispered.

The steps moved away, but no one moved.

After several long minutes, Gracie whispered, "If we stay here and he finds us, we're trapped. Is there another way out?"

Cameron shook his head. "No. I do have other places we can go, but first we need to assess where he is."

Gracie quirked an eyebrow at him.

"I've lived in WITSEC long enough to recognize the need for hiding spots."

"Okay." She nodded.

"The sound reverberates out here. However, I think there's only one shooter."

"Agreed."

"Makes it appear he's everywhere and nowhere all at the same time."

Gracie shifted. "We should get out of here before he returns."

Cameron touched her arm. "Wait. Don't rush out. He's probably watching for movement."

"Ugh, you're right." Gracie tugged Bane closer. "Where do we go from here?"

"I have a bunker," Cameron blurted out.

"Excellent." Gracie sat upright. "Let's go there."

"Yeah, well that's the hard part." Cameron winced. "It's on the other side of my ranch."

"Which means running toward the shooter."

"Exactly."

Gracie paused. "We should also consider there may be more than one assailant," she said. "The gunfire was sporadic. Could've been a man loading and reloading—they took turns."

"Or holding a gun in both hands."

"Or that."

"Great. I'd hate a lack of enemies or challenges." Cameron grunted, then cringed. "Sorry, I resort to sarcasm when I'm stressed."

Gracie chuckled. "If that's the worst that happens, we're fine."

Cameron studied the marshal. She wasn't what he'd expected on many levels. "We also need to consider wildlife that hunts at night, too." He gestured toward Bane. "Will he bark and give us away?"

Gracie shrugged. "I'll order him to stay quiet, but at the end of the day, he's still a dog."

"Right."

"The assailant will probably wait for us at the ranch, watching for our approach."

"Intending to ambush us," Cameron agreed.

"Yes. We're safer staying in the Badlands tonight. If you have ideas where we can find shelter?" Gracie glanced around. "Not that this isn't great, but we're still too close to the ranch if he gets bored and comes looking for us again." She reached for her phone. "And, of course, I have no cell coverage."

"Welcome to the wilderness, where folks can unplug for a while," Cameron quipped.

"Ugh. I'm sure that's a fantastic feature when you don't have a shooter hunting you down." Gracie pocketed her phone. "I don't have the ammunition we need to hold off more than one shooter. Especially not if they have a lot of firepower."

"Is it possible the person or people are part of your gun-trafficking ring?" Cameron considered the words. Maybe the shooters weren't after him, but were hunting her?

"I'd love to say no, but honestly, I have no idea." She scooted back, leaning against the stone wall.

"Maybe they're aware you're here conducting the interviews you mentioned?"

Gracie shook her head, slowly stroking Bane's fur. "Doubtful."

"They could've followed you to my place."

"Your attacker called you by your real name."

Cameron rested his head against his knees. "What if they're not the same attackers, though? If the first guy took off and the others followed you to the ranch..."

"Like you said. Great. I'd hate having a lack of enemies to contend with." She groaned. "Okay, we need to stay hidden and alive until morning. My teammate will arrive to help, and we'll get back to cell reception."

"Agreed."

Without further gunfire, Cameron asked, "Think he or they are finally gone?"

"I hope so," Gracie said.

They inched toward the mouth of the cave, careful to stay to the side, and exited.

Surveying their surroundings, Cameron spotted the bouncing of a soft yellow glow. "Flashlight," he whispered, squinting and deciding it was a single light.

"We go in the opposite direction," Gracie said.

Together, they crept through the foliage, ducking behind bushes, trees and boulders, and moving away from the assailants and the ranch.

When they reached a flat-topped butte, offering a higher vantage point, they spotted a single light bouncing below. No matter which way they went, the pursuer kept in step, gaining on them.

"How is he tracking us?" Gracie asked.

"I don't know." Cameron glanced at Bane. "Could he have a dog?"

"It's certainly possible."

Bane offered a low growl, whether in warning or agreement, Cameron was unsure. Gracie quickly quieted the dog.

"We have to keep going." Cameron scoured his mind, mentally roving the area, and landed on a place he'd almost forgotten about. "I've got it. There's just one issue."

"Oh, good, I'd hate for it to be too easy," Gracie deadpanned.

Cameron grinned—he liked her moxie and personality. "We'll have to cross a creek."

"That doesn't sound awful."

They hurried down the sandy trail, where the foliage was thicker, leading to the vein of water.

When they reached the area, he realized his mistake. It was larger than he'd anticipated, and they required the log that would provide them a way to cross. But it had fallen away, leaving the span too wide, and the ravine was too steep to scale.

In his peripheral vision, the flashlight drew closer.

They'd have to make their way down the ravine. How would Bane keep up?

"We can still do this, but it'll require us to move toward the man following us."

They paused and Gracie turned to look in the direction of the approaching flashlight.

Cameron said, "I know it's a risk, but the place will conceal us."

Gracie gave a quick nod. "Then I trust your judgment."

The words were so simple, and yet they stirred Cameron in a way he couldn't explain. He'd only been responsible for himself for the past twelve years, alone and self-absorbed. Yet, with Gracie at his side, an unfamiliar protective urge overcame him. Not like the concern he had for his employees. It was deeper. Primal. Instinctive.

They scurried farther up the creek, finding the narrow passage of rock, which allowed them to cross. The cold water seeped into his boots, sending a shiver up his spine.

When they reached the opposite side of the creek, they crawled up the tapering ravine and onto the tabled ground above.

The hairs on the back of Cameron's neck rose in visceral response, and he turned to see the flashlight following them across the water.

No time to deal with it. They had to get to safety.

Dependent upon the shadows to protect them, Cameron led Gracie westward. He'd walked this path many times over the two years he'd lived in the area and felt certain he'd find the spot again.

Yet, surveying the mustard-yellow-and-pink layered ridge line surrounded by bushes, sagebrush and prickly flowering plants, he wondered if he'd made a huge mistake. Cameron glanced at Bane, concerned whether the dog could climb.

When he at last spotted the thick rock spires standing like two pillars of a sanctuary, he exhaled his relief. "We're almost there."

They reached the tight crevice, where a hollowed-out log was wedged between the stone.

At Gracie's skeptical expression, Cameron said, "There's more room in there than first appears. It's a snug squeeze at first, then the log opens into a cave. Can Bane make the climb?"

"Definitely," Gracie replied without hesitation.

He'd ask her more about the dog's agility when they were safe. Cameron placed his hands on the rock wall and inched toward the side, pulling himself up to the next level. The strange stair-step pattern positioned a few feet off the ground required them to edge between a set of prickly bushes and through the massive log.

"There's a larger opening at the end."

Gracie nodded and did as he asked while Cameron peered through the foliage, watching the glow of the flashlight approaching. He followed Gracie and Bane, emerging on the other side.

The duo stood at the farthest end of the circular space, sheltered with an open top, exposing them to the elements but inaccessible from the ground because of the surrounding tall spires.

"This is amazing," Gracie whispered.

"Yes, and unless you know to look for it, they won't find us," Cameron said, hoping he was telling the truth. They stood opposite the log opening, ears tuned to every sound.

After what felt like hours, Cameron started to relax, believing the attacker gave up.

Footsteps scraped outside their hiding place, debunking his assumption and filling him with terror.

THREE

Gracie kept Bane close beside her. As though sensing the urgency and seriousness of the moment, the dog thankfully remained silent. She and Cameron exchanged worried glances and neither dared to breathe.

She reconsidered her ammunition. Surprising the assailant was possible if she attacked at the right time. Without a good handle on the danger, Gracie was uncertain of her next steps. Normally, she'd send Bane out first. But they could easily shoot him, and Gracie wouldn't endanger her dog.

Waiting it out was their best option.

The footfalls shifted, as though their attacker was pacing. Or was there more than one? Gracie wasn't sure and without that knowledge, exposing their hiding place put them at risk.

Ready to ambush? Or had they lost the trail?

After what felt like an eternity, there was complete silence.

Gracie exhaled, but her relief was short-lived when the footsteps returned outside the cave entrance confirming whoever shot at them, had also tracked them to the hiding place. Gracie glanced at Cameron. She'd assured him that she trusted him to find them a safe place, and she'd meant it. But with the threat too close for comfort, she second-guessed her decision.

She looked up, spotting the open area overhead. The tall rock surrounding them was too steep to climb, leaving only the hollowed-out log as a means of escape.

It also meant they were trapped.

A thousand scenarios stampeded through Gracie's mind.

Again, Gracie surveyed the tall rock formations that embraced them in the bowl-shaped area. Hidden and yet exposed at the same time. She was certain the assailant couldn't climb up the outside and peer down, but if he found a way to block the entrance, they were trapped.

Cameron shook his head as though interpreting her thoughts. She withdrew her gun, aiming at the log opening. Her heart thudded against her rib cage with such intensity that it drowned out all other sounds.

Please, Lord, don't let Bane bark and alert our location. She kneeled beside the animal, holding up her hand to reiterate the command.

Time seemed to stand still. How long would the person linger before he figured out they were hiding inside the space?

At last, the footsteps moved away, eventually fading.

Gracie dared to exhale, but none of them moved, as they waited for confirmation it was safe.

When the silence dragged on without any further incidents, Gracie whispered, "Think he's gone?"

"I'll check," Cameron whispered.

"No," she argued, moving toward the log. She faced Bane, "Stay—guard." Then, she lifted her hand, reiterating the quiet command again. Bane shifted positions, standing on all fours, focused on the task. "Bane will protect you and I'll return as quickly as possible."

"No. I'll go," Cameron insisted.

"I'm armed."

"But Bane will listen to you before he'll obey me."

Gracie considered that, and it was true. Though she'd instructed the dog not to move, if there was gunfire, she couldn't guarantee Bane wouldn't abandon his post to protect her. That was his first instinct.

"Plus, I know the area better," Cameron added.

"Okay," she acquiesced, and they traded places. "Bane, sit." The dog immediately obeyed but remained upright and on alert beside her.

Cameron crawled into the mouth of the log.

When his boots disappeared, Gracie reconsidered her decision. If she lost the witness or he wound up dead, she and Bane would be trapped in the space and alone in the wilderness without their guide.

She took a step forward, intending to follow Cameron's lead, when he backed out, feet first.

"All clear," he said triumphantly. "The guy gave up, but he wore a path in front of the prickly bushes. Saw the last of the flashlight headed in the direction of my ranch."

"Which also means we can't return there," Gracie concluded.

"Yeah." Cameron's happiness faded slightly. "Wait, this is a safe place to stay."

Gracie turned to look at the confined area. "We have no food or water. We can't start a fire to stay warm, either."

"Agreed, but he won't find us in here. I think we just proved that. We have no idea how long he'll wait at the ranch or where he'll stop along the way."

Gracie sighed. The Badlands were a beautiful tourist attraction, but the canyons and dry landscape didn't provide an abundance of ways for them to survive. And truthfully, not that she'd admit it to Cameron, that wasn't her strong suit.

"We'll wait for daylight and make our way back. Hopefully, by then he'll have given up. And at least we'll be able to see."

Gracie couldn't argue with him. She had no better solution. "Okay, but we leave at first light."

"Agreed."

They settled on the dirt floor. Moonlight poured from above, providing ambient light for them, and the night air was warm and dry.

"Bane, relax," Gracie said. The dog shifted to lie down beside her and began panting softly.

"He's amazing," Cameron said.

"Yes. He's a great partner." She stroked the dog's fur. "You mentioned a bunker?"

Cameron sat and pulled his legs in toward his body, resting his forearms on top of his knees. "I'm never in one place long. After the first year of owning the ranch, I built a bunker at the edge of my property. Figured it was a great hideout should the need arise." Cameron grunted and lowered his head. "Of course, that was before the bad guy ran me off my land."

"Still, you were wise to locate other hiding places," Gracie commended.

"Unfortunately, living like this has developed my oversensitive self-awareness and survival instincts."

Gracie nodded, not wanting to interrupt him.

"I've learned to never become compliant or get too comfortable. And that's where I messed up."

"How so?"

"After years of no major problems or interactions with the senator or dangerous situations, I assumed I was safe. Figured the guy finally gave up on me." Cameron met her gaze and sorrow lingered in his expression. "It was nice to have a reprieve from looking over my shoulder all the time. At some point, shouldn't I be allowed to live without fear?"

"Yes, you should," Gracie said quietly. Grateful the shadows partially concealed her face, she contemplated whether to share her past. If she were to become his handler, she'd need to build trust with him. But Gracie was a temporary protector for him and sharing anything personal developed a bond. She'd gone that route once before in a similar situation, and Rod had shattered her heart. Danger brought on emotional changes in a primitive need for survival. Keeping a professional distance was essential.

"I can't imagine leaving the ranch," Cameron said, oblivious to her thoughts. "Am I going to be forced off my land? Again."

Gracie shook off her worries and sat up straighter. "I hope not, but I can't say for sure. If the senator's people found you, it's not safe for you to remain there."

Cameron snorted bitterly. "If I'd have known this was coming, I might've sold the place when I had the option and at least made a profit."

"It's prime real estate," Gracie said, then added, "At least based on my limited knowledge."

"Oh, yeah. I've had jaw-dropping offers," Cameron admitted. "One guy was so persistent, he promised an unimaginable amount. But owning Pronghorn Hills is more than a job for me. I put my heart and soul into building the cabins and keeping up the grounds. I never considered any of the proposals. Now I'm wondering if that was a huge mistake."

The information bounced around in Gracie's mind. "That's interesting. Tell me more."

Cameron blinked. "What's to tell?"

"Would any of those buyers be willing to kill for the land?"

"What? No." Cameron snorted. "It's not like there's oil or something valuable in the ground."

Gracie wasn't entirely convinced that was true. She made a mental note to check into this eager buyer. "Well, as my dad would've said, don't throw your hands up in surrender just yet. First, let's get out of his situation." Gracie gestured wide with her arms. "Then we will figure out who is behind these attacks and develop a plan of action."

"I'd love to be optimistic, but living more of life in WITSEC, than out of it, I think I left that gene behind. 'Close calls,'" he used his fingers to make air quotes, "that required me to move with little or no notice over the years have left me a little jaded."

"Were the threats credible?"

"Dunno." Cameron shrugged. "I'm still alive. That's gotta say something, right?"

Gracie grinned. She liked Cameron's quick wit and dry sense of humor. "We'll do our best to find out who is doing this." She knew better than to promise they'd take down the assailant. "It doesn't mean you'll have to move."

At Cameron's skeptical glance, she said, "Well… not yet, anyway. Thanks to your quick thinking, we're safe here."

He shrugged, but Gracie noticed his demeanor shifted and he didn't seem as defeated. "It's easier to spot the shooter with his flashlight in the dark, but that also means the nocturnal wildlife sees us better than we can see them."

Gracie swallowed hard. "I hadn't considered that."

"It behooves us to remain in place."

"No arguments here." Gracie attempted to get comfortable but there weren't many options. She sat with her back against the shale and her legs stretched out in front of her. Bane snuggled beside her, resting his head on her thigh with a long sigh. "I think he's ready for a nap." She ran her fingers through his short fur, comforted by her canine partner.

"I've heard Belgian Malinois were wild," Cameron said as he stretched out in a similar position. His boot accidentally hit the top of Gracie's in the process. "Sorry, didn't mean to do that."

"No worries. Bane is not your typical Malinois." Gracie stroked the velvety spot behind the dog's ears. "He's got the high drive, but he's also content to chill after a long day."

"We had lots of dogs growing up in Wyoming. I'd love to adopt one, but uprooting them on a whim isn't fair to the animal."

"Or a human," Gracie mused. "I'm sorry for the stress you've endured. Especially since none of it is your fault."

"Thanks. I'm sure it'll get better someday."

"Are you?"

"Not really."

Gracie chuckled. "Tomorrow we'll tackle your case with gusto."

A deep rumble in the distance interrupted their conversation.

"That wasn't—" Cameron's words were interrupted by the brilliant flash that split the night sky.

An impending thunderstorm would certainly make their night interesting, without shelter.

Gracie looked at Cameron. "I guess we needed one more challenge tonight."

Cameron looked at the log, contemplating the space. "We could huddle in there if necessary."

"I realize it's dead, but isn't it still a tree drawing attention to lightning?"

"Sorta."

"Then, negative," Gracie replied.

"Right. It's not a great option." Cameron shook his head. "Ugh, it would be nice to get a little break for once."

The smell of rain filled the air, and the wind howled, sweeping in the storm.

"Let's hope it's a quick shower passing through."

"If the assailant is out there, he won't be for long," Cameron said.

"I'm not sure which is worse. Waiting here and getting drenched, or taking our chances out there and getting shot," Gracie grumbled.

As though in response, another spear of lightning, jagged and electric, split the sky.

The clouds opened up, releasing a deluge.

When a bolt seemed to strike outside the space, Bane barked. Gracie got to her feet. "We have to find someplace else."

Cameron didn't have a chance to respond as the duo hurried past him. He racked his memory for another location, remembering the corner cave. But the thought of being in the confining space made his skin crawl.

He followed Gracie, and without another plan, they hurried through the log into the night. Cameron was taken aback by a strong gust of wind that made the torrential rainfall pelt him from a sideways angle, piercing his face. The strength of the storm impeded their efforts to seek cover.

Cameron aimed for the corner cave. With the powerful gusts and sheets of rain, he could hardly see in the darkness. Unsure which direction they were headed, he hoped he was leading them correctly. Another bolt of lightning ignited in the sky, providing the flash Cameron needed to spot the landmark he was searching for.

"This way!" he cried against the wind.

Pressing on, they reached the opening and crawled between the stones, entering the pitch-black cave, which was wide in front, then narrowed toward the back. Cameron shivered. This was his last-resort option. He hated tight spaces and had never ventured farther into the cavern. He couldn't handle being confined for any length of time and hoped the storm passed. His mom would've said to pray, but Cameron had given up talking to God a long time ago.

This was as good as Cameron could offer at the moment, so long as Gracie didn't intend going deeper into the cave's bowels.

Wind screeched through the fissure, erupting in a creepy howl. Nature's way of reminding them that it was unpredictable and fearsome. Yet, their choices were dwindling.

They huddled away from the entrance, where the wind and rain whipped unmercifully outside.

Cameron needed a diversion before the urge to be free of the confining space overwhelmed him. The last thing he wanted to do was show his greatest fear and weakness to an attractive female marshal. "So…tell me about yourself. How long have you been a marshal?"

"Since my early twenties."

He nodded. "Were you always a dog handler?"

"No, but I have always loved animals. Bane's my first, and we were partnered about two years ago. He's fantastic."

So the dog was her first K-9. Interesting. She must be in her early thirties, if that.

"Did you grow up around cops? Is that why you chose law enforcement?" Cameron asked.

"No. My folks were big into philanthropy. My mom was a professional event planner."

Not even close to what Cameron had envisioned. "Wow, that threw me."

Gracie smiled as she snuggled with Bane. "Why?"

"I figured your dad was a cop and you followed his footsteps. Your folks are probably proud of you."

Several silent seconds passed between them, and Cameron got the distinct impression he'd overstepped some invisible boundary.

"They were."

Were. Past tense.

Before he could ask, she continued, "Actually, our family had our own personal interaction with the US Marshals and that's what drew me to the vocation."

Cameron waited, his curiosity piquing. When she didn't elaborate, he blurted, "You can't leave me in suspense. I want to hear the rest of this."

Gracie shrugged and sighed. "My kid sister, Leigh, witnessed a murder."

That got his full attention. What were the chances? "Seriously?"

"Yep."

"Are you allowed to talk about it?"

"Oh, yeah. The case was tried a long time ago."

Cameron scooted closer, his earlier claustrophobia dissipating.

"My sister and I had traveled with my parents to an event my mom's company was hosting in Denver. We were elated because they did numerous fundraising efforts, and often, we were left behind when they traveled. We accompanied them this time. Leigh and I were thrilled and wanted to experience everything."

The wind kicked up stronger and they both paused to look at the entrance of the cave as though it would provide some detailed explanation. When it didn't, Gracie continued. "Toward the end of the evening, Leigh was tired and cranky. My parents permitted me to escort her to our room, since it was on the upper floor of the same hotel."

"How old were you?"

"Leigh was nine and I was fifteen." Gracie pulled her knees up to her chest, resting her elbows on them. "On our way, Leigh got a second wind and begged to snoop around the hotel. Since I was in charge, I agreed. I figured it would be a fun adventure for us. We took our time and, of course, then Leigh needed to use the restroom. We found a public restroom at the far end of a long corridor between a connecting event center. I walked ahead of Leigh who had paused at something in the hallway. She said two people were in the shadows. I urged her to hurry up and sneak past without interrupting them. But then we heard the muffled pop of a silencer, and the man nearly ran us over escaping. Turns out, he shot another man, and both were part of a major drug cartel."

"Oh, wow," Cameron said. "And since he'd seen you—"

"Actually, he and Leigh made eye contact. I never saw his face. Anyway, we ran for our lives and escaped unharmed. When we told our parents and the police, things got really complicated. Because of the cartel connection, the authorities felt it was best if we were put under Witness Protection until the man was sentenced."

"You've literally walked a day in my shoes," Cameron said.

"Yes. We weren't sure how long we'd be stuck in that position. Fearing the worst, we anticipated it would be years by the time the killer went through the court system. Turns out, he was murdered in jail. Apparently, the cartel didn't want any loose ends left, either. We were released. But during that time, the marshals treated us with kindness. It stuck with me. Once that happened, all I wanted was to become a marshal and extend that same assistance to others experiencing the trauma we had endured."

A new level of respect for Gracie filled Cameron. She didn't offer platitudes as the others had, pretending they cared when they could go home at the end of the day and spend the time with their family and friends.

"Thank you for sharing with me," Cameron said. "Wait, you said your parents *were* proud of you. Did the cartel return?"

"No, Leigh and my parents were traveling to Maine for my mom's job. The person throwing the event had chartered them a private plane. They were killed in a crash on the way there."

Talk about unfair. "I'm sorry."

"Me, too. But I believe I'll see them again someday. God is my constant peace and support."

Cameron stiffened at the words. "You seriously buy that?" The words tasted bitter in his mouth.

"I do. I take it by your earlier reaction when I was on the phone and just now, you don't."

Cameron didn't want to discuss religion. "I didn't mean to walk in on a private conversation," he said, redirecting the discussion. "I'm curious about the child you were talking about. Your daughter?"

He was probing for personal information.

"Joy's not mine. Recently, our team had a strange event happen. A toddler, less than two years old, was abandoned outside our headquarters building. She was left with only a note—claiming she was related to our leader—and her redacted birth certificate. Daniel, DGTF team leader, is currently searching for her family and any connections she has to him."

Cameron considered the information. "I can't imagine somebody just walking away from a defenseless child."

"There had to be a good reason," Gracie said. "She didn't appear to be mistreated or abused, although sometimes those signs aren't seen on the outside."

"Are there reasons for everything? Sometimes humans are horrible."

"I suppose we lean toward the explanation of a higher purpose for pain and suffering. Working in law enforcement, I've witnessed too much depravity in society. To keep from becoming jaded, I hold on to the fact that there's more than what we see."

"Is that how you felt when your sister witnessed the murder, and you were thrust into WITSEC?"

"No. At first, I was angry they took me away from my friends and our family had to hide because of something we didn't do. None of it was our fault. We were at the wrong place at the wrong time." She looked at him. "But you totally get that."

Cameron hung his head, humbled at her understanding.

"When they apprehended the killer and he subsequently died in prison, I realized we'd helped take a criminal off the streets. We stood up for what was right."

Now, Cameron ruminated on her words. "I never thought about it that way. I focused on the unfairness that the criminal should pay, not the one who did what was right."

"I understand," Gracie replied. "What happened to you was out of your control, forcing you into hiding."

"You're the first marshal who's said that to me." Her words lingered in his mind. Could he look at his life differently? He'd contributed to the greater good by taking Quigley off the streets and away from his political corruptions. He would've affected many innocent people if he'd been reelected. "It sounds like Joy's mother is in a bad situation," Cameron said, again redirecting the conversation.

"That's what we're surmising, as well. There must be a reason she'd leave her child behind. If it was to protect her, then I can't judge her. Although there might've been smarter ways to handle it." Gracie shifted positions and the scent of her sweet perfume wafted toward Cameron. "Before you became Cameron Holmes, who was James Dunwood?"

Cameron sighed. How long had it been since he'd thought about the family ranch? "I grew up on four-hundred-acres in Wyoming. I had always planned to inherit it and continue our family business."

She nodded, encouraging him to continue.

"My parents were wonderful people," Cameron replied. "I was an only child, more by medical circumstance than choice. I think they would have had ten children if they'd had the option. I often wished I had siblings, especially when I was put into Witness Protection. There's nothing worse than being completely alone with nobody to talk to, no friends who understand you, nobody that you can turn to and depend on."

Gracie nodded, but she didn't reply, and he cringed inwardly at his insensitivity.

"What reasoning is there for your family's deaths?"

Gracie blinked and her expression sobered. Cameron instantly regretted his words. Why had he asked that?

"I believe God's in control, even when bad things happen to good people. Maybe there isn't always an explanation this side of eternity, or the question is too big for us to answer."

"I think you're the smartest person I've ever met," Cameron replied.

Gracie laughed. "You need to get out more."

"No significant others?" Cameron blurted. What was wrong with him? Her personal life was none of his business. She was a marshal doing her job and not even his handler. Not that he'd been friends with them. They were cops who popped in and out of his life to check on him. More like having a disinterested babysitter.

"Not anymore," Gracie replied. "What about you?"

"It's hard to date when you're unsure if or when you'll have to move or change your name. It's impossible to be in a real relationship when you can't be truthful about who you really are. You can't be vulnerable with them." He paused, confused at his honest response. Images of his short-lived interactions with Delilah returned and he shoved them away.

Again, a long moment of silence hung between them. He'd not meant to come off like a jerk, but the question irritated a raw spot in his heart.

A cry echoed from the narrowed part of the cave.

Realization tackled him as Gracie scooted to her feet. "Cameron…don't mountain lions make their dens inside caves?"

FOUR

Gracie didn't wait for Cameron's response. She grabbed Bane's leash and hurried out of the mouth of the cave. Whatever was inside the deeper recesses wouldn't appreciate their invasion. She'd take her chances in the thunderstorm.

Fortunately, the rain was dissipating, and they trudged over the softened earth again in search of a place to hide out.

Cameron turned to look behind them. "Yeah, that wasn't the wisest move," he admitted.

"It worked for a while," Gracie said. "Got any other ideas?" How long could they wander in the Badlands?

"I do. But we'll have to hike farther into the park and away from the ranch."

As if they had so many other options. "Lead on."

Mist replaced the droplets as they hiked through the forested areas. "This is pretty," Gracie said. Trees and rocks were interspersed in the sandy area, giving it less of a desert ambiance.

"Uh-huh." Cameron's half-hearted reply told Gracie he wasn't interested in talking.

Too bad. She wanted information about how someone had discovered his identity. If Cameron played any part in that, she'd find out.

Making a second attempt, she said, "I never considered how WITSEC controls your life, including relationships."

"Don't get me wrong. I am grateful for all your office has done in providing and protecting me. I'd just also like to have an authentic life that didn't involve living solo forever." Cameron exhaled. "Having that thug call me by name is unnerving and reiterates I'm stuck being alone."

"It also leads credence to that person being someone from your past."

"Maybe."

"If not from your past, then let's talk about your present. Have you experienced friendships or romantic interests gone wrong that might expose who's after you?"

He stopped in his tracks and faced her. "Now, you're blaming me for someone trying to kill me?"

"Absolutely not."

Cameron spun on his heel and continued walking. After several minutes, he replied, "Every relationship I have is superficial. How can it be anything less?"

"I can't imagine," Gracie replied softly. "You've sacrificed everything with no end in sight. I suppose those in charge of WITSEC failed to connect the bridge between the goal of survival with the people's everyday lives that it affects."

"It stinks," Cameron admitted. "Joel Iverson owns a guest ranch like mine. Aside from my employees, he's my closest friend."

Gracie's ears perked. A competitor had motive for removing Cameron. Not wanting to put him on the defensive again, she hesitated to probe about Joel but made a mental note to ask Cheyenne Chen, the technical analyst on the task force, to check him out.

Her silence paid off because Cameron said, "The one time I got involved with someone, she turned out to be…a little unstable."

That got her full attention. Gracie paused. "Now this, I gotta hear," she eventually said.

"I met Delilah at a local coffee shop. We accidentally received the other's order and started talking. I spent a little more time hanging out there after exchanging our drinks. She was sweet."

Was. Unstable. Key words Gracie homed in on. "And?"

"We went out on a couple of dinner dates. Nothing spectacular. She was fun."

"I appreciate suspense as much as the next woman, but I'm hoping there's more to this."

He groaned. "I don't know. There was something about her that gave me strange vibes."

"Like?"

"Delilah's interest in my daily activities bordered on…"

"Stalking?"

"I dunno, that's harsh. She was…a little clingy."

Gracie tried not to roll her eyes. Great. The woman showed interest and Cameron flipped out on her. "Let me guess, instead of telling her you weren't interested, you ghosted her."

"Not at first. I tried both—neither worked. She wasn't peeping through my windows at night, she was just persistent."

"And? Cameron, I need details. Anyone you've interacted with has the potential to be a suspect right now. If Delilah had you in her sights, is it possible she discovered your true identity?"

"I seriously doubt that. How could she?"

"Did she ever stalk you? Enter your home uninvited?"

They trudged up a deep ravine, neither speaking until they reached the top.

"Delilah left flowers or small gifts outside my office during the night."

"You have a security gate. Unless you gave her the code, that qualifies as trespassing."

"Except I couldn't prove she'd done it. There were no cards or identifiers. When I asked Delilah, she played it off."

"Do you have cameras set up around your cabin?"

"No." His quick answer had Gracie wondering if that, too, was a sore spot. "Cameras are a double-edged sword. People come here with an expectation of getting away from it all."

"Good point." His hesitation had her wondering what he was hiding. "Cameron, I'm not here to judge you. I am fact-finding." She cleared her throat. "Reading people's body language is an important skill in my line of work. What aren't you telling me?"

"When Joel discovered I was seeing Delilah, he warned me away from her. He said his buddy had dated her a year or so prior, and she'd done some sketchy things afterward. She doesn't take rejection well, so he warned me to be careful about separating myself from her. He claimed she had a history of overreacting."

"Interesting."

"And Delilah knew about your daily activities?"

"Yep."

"Does she have a new love interest? Is she playing the jealousy game by using her new beau to create problems with you?"

"What good would that do?"

"I've seen stranger behavior. She might want you to fight for her so she's testing to see how much you care."

"Doubtful."

Something in Cameron's tone had Gracie pondering if he was withholding information. "I'd still like to hear specifics."

Cameron exhaled an exasperated sigh. "She would call and leave voicemail messages—'I saw that you bought steaks at the supermarket this weekend. Are you making a romantic dinner for somebody?' Stuff like that."

"Yikes," Gracie said.

"Tell me about it. She's peculiar."

"How did you finally get rid of her?"

"I haven't. I ignore her."

Gracie's mental wheels turned. Would this woman take jealous revenge by trying to kill Cameron? Regardless, that didn't explain whether she'd figured out his real identity. Unless... Had Cameron revealed it to her and was now hiding his mistake? "Would she be involved with the attack?"

Cameron snorted. "She's no assassin—she's obsessive."

"Never underestimate the power of a woman scorned or determined. Most women incarcerated are there for crimes of passion."

"We didn't date long enough to form a bond."

They reached a formation of several massive rocks.

"Hopefully this will work for the rest of the night," Cameron said, diverting the conversation. He helped Gracie and Bane up toward a thick mass of greenery. "Shelter is in there."

They crawled through the small opening, concealed by foliage. Gracie used her flashlight to illuminate the space. Wood planks created a room no larger than a coat closet, width-wise, and not tall enough to stand in. The confining space didn't give them ample room to move, but it had overhead shelter and a dirt floor. Most importantly, the branches and bushes hid them from the shooter. In the corner, Cameron retrieved a few bottles of waters. "I'm short on supplies."

"Please pour some into my hands so Bane can drink."

Cameron did as she asked and Bane lapped greedily at the liquid, consuming two handfuls before settling beside her. Cameron passed her the bottle he held.

"I'm fine."

"Take it, please," he insisted. "I'll finish Bane's bottle."

"Okay. Thank you. Let's hope the shooter gave up and returned to the rock he'd crawled out from under."

"Most likely he did. Especially when the storm hit."

"Still, it's better we stay here until morning," Gracie advised.

"Agreed."

Gracie couldn't stop thinking about Delilah's possible involvement. Jealousy was a solid motive for murders committed by women. "Let's resume our discussion about Delilah."

"Must we? I thought we covered that topic."

"Hear me out. If jealousy is a factor for her, and she has a history of entering your office uninvited, could she have looked at your guest list and seen my name? You said you'd cleared your reservations. She might find that suspicious and assumed I'd be alone on the property with you. She could've become enraged?"

Cameron shrugged. "I suppose it's possible."

"I'll run her when we get back to civilization."

"Do what you got to do," he said disinterestedly.

"I have to ask one more thing."

Cameron pinned her with an irritated stare, visible even in the dim light. "At any point, did you reveal your real name to Delilah? Even accidentally or inadvertently, when you weren't on guard?"

He snorted and shook his head. "No."

"I'm not accusing you. I want to make sure we're looking at all viable suspects."

"Gracie, I've lived almost as much of my life in WITSEC as I did outside of it. I'm aware of the rules."

"Excellent. Never hurts to keep an open mind. Sometimes it's the people closest to a victim who are responsible."

"Exactly why relationships are out of the question for me. I keep a distance from everyone. And I'm good at it." Sadness hovered in his tone. "Aside from the fact that my life is a lie, I cannot pick someone stable to sustain a relationship with. It just wouldn't work." He looked down. "Romance isn't in my future, at least not until I'm released from WITSEC. I can't pretend to be somebody else. It's unfair and deceptive to the woman."

"I suppose you're right." In a way, he was protecting himself, and Gracie understood that survival technique well after all that happened with Rod. Though he was the last topic she'd want to talk about. Keeping him off her mind was hard enough. Not because she wanted him back, but because she couldn't stop replaying how she'd missed all the signs. But she realized how vulnerable Cameron had been telling her about his experience. Perhaps reciprocating would start to earn his trust.

"I can empathize. I was involved with a guy who I thought was the one. Why do we always say that?" she asked with a snort. "'The one.' Like there's a single option for each person and if you miss it, 'oh, well.' Do you believe that?"

"No," Cameron said. "I mean, I guess I don't know. I feel bad if there's one for me because she's out there wandering around and I'm stuck in Witness Protection and can't get to her."

Gracie laughed. She loved his personality and the way he tossed out dry humor to keep things light. It was almost as though he instinctively sensed when she'd need it. "That's one way to look at it."

"So what happened?"

She sighed. "After losing my family, I kept to myself, worked as every available hour of overtime. Basically, anything to stay occupied." Forgetting her dreams of a husband, children, and a normal life outside of work. She shrugged off the thoughts. That future belonged to someone else, right? Not everyone got a happily-ever-after. "And that's exactly where I went wrong and met him."

"Does 'him' have a name?"

She chuckled. "Rod. I'd never been in an emotional place where I trusted somebody wholeheartedly. I'd always maintained my guard, which is common for cops. It's kind of a job hazard. We live with a constant undercurrent of suspicion."

"Maybe I was destined to be a cop. I'm right there with you."

She smiled.

"But you let down your guard," Cameron surmised.

"Yes, I did. He was working on a fugitive case with me. Since he's also in law enforcement, I assumed we had a mutual understanding and respect for honesty. And that was my biggest mistake."

"He broke your heart."

"Yes." Gracie swallowed hard, not wanting to talk about Rod anymore. "See? Clearly, you're not alone. I have no better record of picking people than you do." She attempted to laugh to disguise the pain. The sound was hollow, and she wondered if Cameron heard the bitterness behind her words. Thankfully, he didn't press for her to elaborate. Some things were too raw to expose to a stranger.

As comfortable as she felt around Cameron, she reminded herself that's exactly what they were. Strangers.

They talked for several hours, passing the time with stories of their childhoods. The levity helped Gracie relax as she regaled him with stories of her and Leigh's antics. Cameron confessed how much he missed being authentic. She enjoyed talking to him, and Gracie felt that unfamiliar spark of attraction. She shoved it down, reminding herself they'd both staked their ground and firmly established that their partnership in his life-saving mission was purely work-related. Neither of them was romance material.

But as they grew tired, and she closed her eyes, Gracie couldn't help but feel a little disappointed. Cameron was the first man she'd been around who was the total package. Smart, funny, a great conversationalist and knock-your-shoes-off handsome, with his dark hair and blue eyes. They'd talked as though they'd known one another their entire lives. She'd never felt that way with anyone, even Rod.

Too bad. In another place, time and world, they might've been good together. Gracie reminded herself in their present circumstances, her duty was to keep Cameron alive.

Her body relaxed and she allowed herself to drift off.

A scraping had Gracie bolting upright, heart drumming and ears tuned into her surroundings. Had she imagined it? She flicked a glance at Bane, who sat stoic, ears perked. "You heard it, too?"

Gracie remained still for at least half an hour with no further incident. Cameron slept peacefully, leaning against the stone wall in what had to be the most uncomfortable position ever.

The beginning of sunrise permitted ambient light, allowing her to see Cameron better. His dark eyelashes—long and lush, the kind that women coveted—fluttered slightly. What was he dreaming about?

She eased into a crawl and inched out of the shelter, pausing to survey their surroundings before exiting completely. Bane stayed close behind her.

Gracie stood upright and stretched to release the stiffness in her back and shoulders. Taking her cue, Bane offered a yawn and accompanying squeak. She scratched him behind the ears, then withdrew her cell phone with her free hand, confirming she still had no reception. She had to reach Zach before he walked into an ambush at the ranch.

Hopefully, the attacker had given up, but she wouldn't assume anything that might get them all killed. She wanted to get moving before the sun fully rose, but before waking Cameron, she'd conduct a little recon to ensure it was safe for them to leave.

They guardedly moved, examining the landscape. Once she'd completed a full circle and returned to the shelter, having seen nothing of concern, she exhaled relief. She'd wake Cameron and they'd start the trek back to the ranch.

Her plan evaporated when Bane stiffened beside her, ears perked.

Gracie paused. Was the killer watching and waiting for her and Cameron to emerge from their hiding place?

Movement in her peripheral had Gracie ducking quickly behind the bush, and she tugged Bane closer.

He jerked against her restraint, and she spotted the white tail of the rabbit bounding in the opposite direction. Gracie grinned, pressing her palm against her pounding heart. "Leave it," she ordered the dog.

To his credit, Bain didn't charge after the creature, but she could see in his tense muscles that he desperately wanted to. "Sorry, buddy. Another time," she promised. Without binoculars or surveillance equipment, they'd have to rely on their senses and proceed with the utmost caution.

Gracie started to duck back into the hiding place when Cameron appeared in the open space. She startled and gasped.

"Sorry, I didn't mean to scare you," Cameron said, unfolding from the crouched position.

"I'm a little on edge."

"Understandably so." He eased to his full height. "That's the most uncomfortable position I've ever slept in in my life."

"Mine, too," she chuckled. Bane offered a quiet grunt and Gracie stroked his neck. "He agrees."

"Think it's safe for us to return to the ranch?" Cameron asked.

"Yes, but carefully," Gracie said, snapping on Bane's leash.

They made their way through the tall stumps of sagebrush and thistles, Bane in the lead, Gracie and Cameron trailing behind.

The early morning light permitted her to better evaluate their situation. Stepping over the cracked clay beds where water once flowed, she noticed the deep fissures and dry ravines. Vibrant ridgeline colors developed the magnificent landscape.

A sweet juniper scent carried in the breeze, which fluttered her hair around her face.

"I never tire of this place. You said you grew up nearby?"

"About an hour north, in Black Hawk," Gracie replied. "I agree, I love it here." She didn't add that was also probably why she'd never left South Dakota; despite the bad memories and tragedies she'd experienced here.

The striped rock formations in shades of red and yellow that surrounded them on every side formed bluffs and enhanced the visual appeal. Birds chirped, filling the background with their symphony.

Cameron paused, placing a hand to hold Gracie back. "What's wrong?" she whispered, instinctively reaching for her gun.

He pointed to the leveled ground in front of them where a male pronghorn stood frozen, fixated on them. The antelope-like buck had reddish-brown fur with a white underside and neck. At the shoulders, she guessed him to be about three feet tall and close to one hundred pounds. The buck's horns were about a foot in length, with distinctive prongs on the front, giving the creature his name.

The quiet moment shattered when Bane barked, sending the pronghorn fleeing in the opposite direction.

Cameron flicked a glance at her.

She shrugged. "At the end of the day, he's still a dog."

He laughed. "That's logical. At least you got to see one."

"They're beautiful animals." She offered a silent prayer of thanks for the momentary reprieve from their current situation.

Cameron led them up the ravine where the pronghorn had stood only moments before.

They traveled an unfamiliar path, and Gracie spotted the evidence of their pursuer's partial boot prints in the ground. "Here," she pointed to them.

Cameron stayed in step with her, following the trail. Gracie gestured to the breaks in the branches and snapped twigs on the forest floor. Neither spoke, enjoying the rejuvenating scenery.

She kneeled near a babbling brook, where the cold clear water ran over the pebble rocks, filling the background with comforting sounds.

Cameron leaned against a hefty boulder and smiled. "Our ranch back in Wyoming had a lot of the same features this place does. I guess that's part of what drew me here," he said. "Especially water sources like this. They were my favorite hangouts as a kid."

"We spent a lot of time in Custer State Park and the Black Hills when I was a kid."

"Both places are beautiful," Cameron agreed. "I have to say, of the many locations I've had to live while in WITSEC, South Dakota is my favorite."

They continued walking, falling into comfortable silence. Gracie found him easy to talk to and she replayed their conversation from the night before.

She'd assured Cameron there was a reason for everything that happened in life, but maybe it was as simple as trusting the wrong guy that had gotten her a broken heart. She'd blamed herself for letting down her guard to a man who didn't deserve her trust or love. What scared her most was accepting she'd been so wrong about Rod. As Cameron had said, he couldn't pick a good one, either. Gracie shook off the feelings, reminding herself that clinging to negative thoughts wasn't helpful. Refocusing on Cameron's case was priority number one.

"Let's concentrate on who could be involved with this. Who wants you dead or who has tracked you down after all these years? What's changed?"

"I've wondered those same things," Cameron admitted. "Quigley and his people have had twelve years to search for me. If they were going to do something, they could have done it a long time ago. Why wait until now? That makes no sense at all."

"Unless they finally found you."

"Right."

"But let's widen the search into more current events. I'll check into Delilah. Are there any other interactions you might've had that created animosity?"

"To the degree that someone wants me dead?" Cameron asked.

"Remember reasons that might seem illogical to us, make perfect sense to the perpetrator."

"Nobody comes to mind."

"What about disagreements or issues with customers or employees?"

"Let me think."

"How about the most recent property buyer you mentioned?" Gracie asked.

"He was pushy, aggressive in a persuasive way, but not threatening. No potential buyers gave me bad vibes." After several minutes, Cameron said, "I fired an employee a couple of months ago."

"Tell me about the situation."

"Arlee Gross worked for me from the starting days of the ranch. Great guy, but he missed a lot of time for personal reasons. Then he started making big mistakes on cabin projects."

"Was he angry when you fired him?"

Cameron paused to face Gracie. The sun crested the horizon, painting the sky with bright pink and purple slashes. "Upset, for sure. He pleaded for me to reconsider because he was behind in child-support payments. The judge had already threatened to revoke his visitation rights if he didn't get them caught up. I wanted to help him, but his blunders nearly got me thrown in court for unsafe accommodations. I couldn't afford to risk my business."

Gracie considered his words. A wronged employee had motive to kill, especially if he'd lost custody or visitation with his child. The devastation would be life-altering. "Okay, I'll look into Arlee Gross, as well."

Cameron took large strides to climb up the rock

formations, then turned, giving Gracie a hand upward. Bane bounded beside her.

"He's part kangaroo," Cameron joked.

"Truly. Malinois are super agile. It's part of the reason the military and law enforcement use them," Gracie said. "Besides Arlee and Delilah, does anyone else come to mind?"

"No, Quigley has always been my biggest enemy."

"What can you tell me about him?"

"He was a real-estate developer who offered to buy our family ranch. At first, he was great to be around, kind and generous. My dad was an environmentalist, and he and my mom were active in several nonprofit organizations that supported naturalism across Wyoming. When they discovered Quigley was dumping illegal chemicals, they figured out his motive behind befriending them."

"He wanted the land."

"Yes, but not with his name on it."

"If I remember correctly, he had several shell corporations where he laundered money."

"Yes. He purchased private acreages then used them to illegally dump the chemicals."

"Why not buy barren land to avoid being caught?" Gracie asked.

"The acreages camouflaged the dumping. His real-estate transactions were in Utah before spreading into Wyoming."

"What did your parents do?" Gracie asked.

"They tried talking to him first, believing they'd get him to confess and report him to the authorities.

He attempted bribery. My parents were true to the core. They believed in the cause, and they refused to be moved by Quigley's deception. They reported him and agreed to testify against him. When he discovered what they'd done, he opted to murder them instead. He says it wasn't premeditated, but he brought a loaded gun to their meeting."

Though Gracie had read facts in the file, hearing the account from Cameron produced a different response.

"You know what's ironic?" Cameron asked. "The prison time Quigley would have served for his environmental offenses would have been less than the murder sentence he received for killing my parents. It's like he failed to weigh the consequences."

"He panicked when he imagined the scandal destroying his political career and ambitions."

"Yep." Cameron shook his head sadly.

"You were only eighteen when this happened?" Gracie asked.

"I missed my senior prom and graduation. Quigley stole all the big coming-of-age events kids look forward to. Not to mention he killed my parents. The only family I had. If anything, shouldn't I be the one seeking revenge on Quigley rather than him coming after me?"

"Good point. Quigley's cronies made continuous attempts on your life?"

"I've moved twice before when your office received credible threats. Never had someone figure out my true identity though. That's new."

"What was the last occurrence?"

"Five years ago. A driveby shooting at my workplace, though your office couldn't connect it directly to Quigley. The occasional death threats, but those might've come from Quigley's voters and not necessarily from him."

"We're keeping him at the top of our suspect list," Gracie replied.

Their trek to the ranch took them through what seemed like endless acres of dry ground. Cameron walked with purpose and confidence. Had it been any other time of year or situation, she pictured their adventure being enjoyable.

They reached the creek they'd crossed the night before and Bane stopped to sniff near the water's edge. Gracie kneeled. "Hey, check this out." She pointed to the partial boot prints in the softened ground.

Cameron moved to her side and inspected the tracks. "I would've totally missed those. Great job, Bane."

The dog's tail swished with appreciation.

"Only one set."

"One shooter," Gracie said. "Hey, we made the smartest choice possible based on the evidence we had at the time. I could've sent Bane after him, but he would've shot my dog."

"I completely agree."

Once they neared the ranch, they performed a perimeter search to ensure there was no one waiting to ambush them. They returned to where Bane had chased the offender to the dirt road, locating a second set of tracks.

"Apparently, this is where the guy likes to park," Gracie replied. "Now we know to watch this area."

"He's not smart. Returns to the scene of the crime," Cameron teased.

"Right."

Gracie heaved a sigh of relief that they'd found no other vehicles on the property. She texted a quick update to Zach, warning him to be on the lookout.

She and Cameron headed for his cabin office and collected the welcome basket for Gracie's cabin. "You still have the key to your cabin from earlier?"

"Yes." She patted her pocket.

"While you freshen up, I'll make breakfast. Head over when you're ready."

"Sounds great," Gracie said.

He led her outside. "I'll walk over if you want to drive your pickup to the cabin."

"No way. Hop in." Gracie unlocked the pickup and loaded Bane while Cameron slid into the passenger seat. The drive was short and when they reached her guest accommodations, Gracie gathered her bag and released Bane.

The porch spanned the quaint rectangular cabin, and the wooden railing created a barrier from the two rocking chairs and a narrow side table. Cameron unlocked the single lock, something Gracie noted wouldn't do much to keep out a killer, and pushed the door open.

A blue-and-white-checkered sofa with matching recliner sat in front of the woodburning fireplace surrounded by a stone wall. A flatscreen TV hung above it, and a two-person dining table separated the kitchenette.

"It's fully stocked with cookware, plates, utensils and basics," Cameron said. "There are logs on the side of the cabin, and fire starters in that box."

At the far end of the room, double French doors stood wide, revealing a single queen-size bed. The open second door showed the bathroom.

"There's towels, sheets and blankets in the linen closet in the bedroom," Cameron explained.

"Wow, it's lovely," Gracie said, meaning every word.

"I'm working to give the other cabins a more modern look, too. It's hard to market rugged cabins to glampers," Cameron chuckled, referencing the urban slang term for glamorous campers.

"Must admit, I'd be in the glamper category." Gracie leaned against the back of the sofa.

"You did great hiding out last evening. No complaints."

"None I voiced to you," she teased.

Cameron laughed. "Touché. Anyway, I'll get out of your hair and let you settle in. Meet at my cabin in an hour?"

"I'll bring my laptop and we can work there."

Cameron nodded and exited the cabin. Gracie watched from the window, noticing a shift in his demeanor. Cameron. The name was too formal for him. Cam. She liked that better. Maybe she'd deploy the nickname and see how he received it.

Bane sniffed her hand.

"Well, buddy, ready for some food?" Gracie asked Bane. She walked to her bag and withdrew his dog food and collapsible bowls, then filled both. The dog snarfed down the meal while Gracie moved to the bathroom. A hot shower rejuvenated her. Once she'd dressed and returned to the living room, a text vibrated her phone from where it sat charging. She glanced at the screen and saw a message from Zach.

Running behind, ETA 0900.

Sounds good, she texted. So far, they'd avoided the danger, but she had a feeling it wouldn't be quiet for long. Whoever was out to get Cameron was determined. But so was Gracie. She'd find the criminal and make sure they paid. Then she and Bane would return to what they did best—apprehending a gun-trafficking ring and the murderers of fellow DGTF member, Plains City Detective Kenyon Graves.

FIVE

A hot shower and fresh clothes did wonders for Cameron's attitude, though he couldn't shake the feeling someone was watching them. He'd lived for quite a while on hypervigilant status and paranoia was second nature. And since they'd conducted recon and not found anyone lurking on the premises, and Gracie hadn't appeared concerned, he stifled the feelings.

For now.

The more pleasant path for his thoughts to travel centered around Gracie, and he allowed himself to ponder. Despite his heart's repetitive warnings that the beautiful deputy marshal was off-limits, and reminders that he wasn't interested in romance, Cameron couldn't get Gracie out of his mind.

The flicker of memory regarding their conversation eliminated the joyful contemplations, since he regretted telling Gracie about Delilah. No doubt, she considered him foolish for getting involved with a local who had seriously unhealthy attachment issues.

Too late now.

He had bigger fish to catch—like the assailant who apparently wanted Cameron dead. If only he understood why, he might have a shot at narrowing down who it was. He'd lived in unceasing fear of the senator and his cohorts. With limitless funds and connections, even behind bars, Quigley had endless options. And until Gracie asked, Cameron never considered he had enemies besides Quigley.

Gracie was a deep thinker, so perhaps she'd come up with something to help them in the investigation. He'd felt empowered when she'd asked his opinion, and Cameron realized he enjoyed the investigative aspects. Though he'd prefer not to be the killer's target. Still, for the first time in his life, Gracie had included him instead of ordering him around. Years of being shuffled in and out of WITSEC identities and locations had infringed on his personal freedom and made him a prisoner to the senator's whims. He'd even stolen Cameron's birth name.

Gracie treated him differently. She came alongside him, sharing the burden, which he appreciated. He grabbed his Sig Sauer from the nightstand and checked the magazine, ensuring it was ready. He wouldn't make the mistake of leaving the premises again without it on hand.

Cameron whistled as he headed into the kitchen, excited at the prospect of demonstrating his culinary skills for Gracie. At last, he'd share a meal with someone instead of cooking for one. He opened the fridge and peered inside.

"Hello, James."

Cameron whipped around, staring at the masked man standing on the other side of the kitchen island. "How'd you get in here?"

In response, the man hoisted a pistol, aiming it at Cameron, and fired.

Diving behind the refrigerator door, Cameron scurried out of the kitchen and into the living room. He crawled around the sofa and returned fire at the intruder who hid behind the kitchen island.

After several shots, loud footfalls faded to the back of the cabin. Cameron emerged and started after the intruder. An open window in one of the bedrooms revealed his entry point, but the man had escaped. An involuntary shiver ran through Cameron at the thought that seconds earlier, the man could've shot him while he showered.

Cameron rushed to the front door and jerked it open.

He froze in place.

A rattlesnake lay coiled on his doormat.

He slammed the door shut, then tucked the Sig into his waistband. Cameron hurried to snag the snake tong catcher from his hall closet. The reptiles weren't a rarity on the ranch, and thankfully, he was prepared for such an occasion. Cameron considered the back window where the intruder had entered. Uncertain if the man watched or planned to shoot again, he opted to climb out his living room window on the other side instead.

Once he'd ensured the intruder had fled, Cameron rounded the cabin, collecting the live trap from the garden shed, and carried both to the front porch.

Using the five-foot-long tong, he carefully captured the unhappy reptile and dropped into the live trap, securing it from escaping.

Bane's sharp barks erupted from the direction of Gracie's cabin.

He was no dog expert, but the sound wasn't playful.

It was a warning.

Had the intruder gone after Gracie?

With the tong and trap in hand, Cameron bolted to Gracie's cabin, fearing what he'd find.

The barking had ceased, which sent his pulse racing. Was he too late?

When he reached her cabin and rounded the structure, he spotted Bane standing at full attention, guarding Gracie, who was frozen inches from her porch steps. Her wide eyes met his.

Cameron spotted the reptile before he heard the rattling tail. Bane stood between the rattler and Gracie, unmoving and silent.

She had a backpack slung over her shoulder and a leg holster revealed her gun. No doubt, she was an excellent shot, but was she experienced in dealing with deadly snakes?

Cameron lifted the supplies in each hand, and Gracie gave an almost imperceptible nod of understanding. He inched toward the reptile, extending the tongs again, and prayed his skills worked a second time. There was no room for mistakes. If he timed it wrong, the snake would either turn on him or lunge for Bane.

"Order Bane to remain still," Cameron said in a low, quiet voice.

"Bane, *bleib*," Gracie repeated.

Cameron assumed the word was German for stay, and he hoped it worked.

He inched closer, the snake's attention on Bane. "Don't move," he said quietly.

Aiming carefully, he grasped the rattler with the tongs. The angered snake whipped against the restraints. Cameron's grip was tight, and he dropped it into the trap.

Gracie visibly relaxed. "Is it safe?"

Cameron surveyed the area. "I don't see any others."

She and Bane took a wide birth around the trap and hurried to Cameron. "Thank you."

"I'll notify the game warden and ask them to remove our visitors." Cameron reached for his cell phone and placed the call. After requesting the assistance to remove the snakes, he turned to Gracie. "They'll come and get them this morning."

"Are we safe to leave that?" Gracie flicked a glance at the box.

"We could carry it back."

She shivered. "Do we have to?"

"Well, unless they're doing snake push-ups, I don't think they'll escape," he assured her teasingly.

"I had a million questions to ask you, but I was scared to breathe," she admitted.

"Yeah, you both were very smart."

"I heard gunshots and came out to assist when I found that." She visibly shivered.

"He got away and left one of those on my doorstep too."

Her mouth fell open. "Cam, you're okay though?"

Cam. Nobody had ever called him by a nickname, and he found it strangely appealing. Shaking off the inappropriate thoughts, he blurted, "Yes, but whoever this guy is, he's determined."

"And creative."

"Right. Keep your eyes out for any others."

"Which means he watched us return here today." Gracie gazed out beyond Cameron, pivoting slowly.

"We'll secure the trap closer to my cabin. I don't want them accidentally roaming my property. That puts us in constant danger." He pointed to her cabin. "Do you need to get anything else from inside?"

"No."

"I'm so glad you came when you did. I wasn't sure what to do. I grew up in South Dakota, but it was as if everything I'd learned about handling rattlesnakes flew out of my brain."

"You did exactly what you should've."

"Do you always keep snake-trapping supplies on hand?" Gracie gestured toward the tongs.

"I rarely see them out here anymore, but it helps to be prepared."

"I'm glad you didn't kill it. It's not that I like

snakes, but I'm not sure how I feel about killing it, either."

"That's why we trap them and hand them over to someone else to make those decisions." Cameron smiled.

"Good."

Cameron hoisted the trap and prong, and they headed for his place. "Bane is incredibly smart to have remained silent and still after ushering that warning bark."

Once they reached his cabin, Cameron closed and locked the door behind them. Then double checked the windows.

"We know for certain that our assailant is nothing if not tenacious." Gracie placed her backpack on the floor and slid into a chair at his dining table.

"He underestimated me. Growing up on a ranch and living out here in the wilderness has provided essential life skills." Cameron moved to the sink, washed his hands and returned to preparing their breakfast. "Normally, we wouldn't bother them if they're not close to the lodging area, but they're a danger if left on the grounds."

"If Bane hadn't spotted it before me, I would've literally walked right into that trap." Gracie shook her head. The dog immediately moved to her side, and she stroked his face. "You're my hero." Bane panted softly in response.

"He would've taken on that snake for you," Cameron said, cracking eggs into a bowl.

"Yes." Gracie's gaze never left the dog, appreciation and love evident in the team's body language.

"That's devotion." Cameron commenced making scrambled eggs and bacon while Gracie withdrew her computer and set up at the table.

"In all fairness, you tackled the reptile for me, too. I guess that makes you also my hero."

Though her tone was teasing, warmth filled Cameron's chest at her appraisal. He focused on finishing their meal and slid a steaming plate in front of Gracie. She pushed aside her laptop, allowing her to work while she ate.

"Zach is running a little behind but should be here soon. In the meantime, let's work on the suspect list," Gracie said, taking a bite. She paused. "Those are the best scrambled eggs I've ever had."

Cameron beamed under her approval. "My secret recipe."

"It's delicious."

"I enjoy having someone to cook for," Cameron admitted.

Understanding passed between them in an unspoken expression. She smiled and Cameron allowed himself to be absorbed in her green irises. How could a single glance make him feel accepted, seen, and cared for? Gracie Fitzgerald's ability to show how much she got Cameron was unmatched.

Knock it off. She's only here temporarily until your new handler shows up. Don't get attached.

He averted his gaze, clearing his throat, and reminded himself that years of solitude had developed his perfect aloofness. He wouldn't become involved with anyone. Especially a woman.

Gracie's presence had him exercising that skill beyond his emotions. He'd have to work overtime around her. And for the first time, he was grateful for the third party coming to assist them.

Once more he considered how the danger had gotten too close. What if the intruder had shot Gracie while Cameron dealt with the snake? Fury boiled his blood. Coming after him was one thing, but hurting Gracie was unconscionable. They had to stop the assailant and fast before their close calls became death sentences.

Gracie averted her eyes from Cameron, inwardly chastising herself for responding to the zing she experienced when he was near. Interfering or fraternizing with a witness wasn't acceptable behavior for a deputy marshal. Especially with her history. Images of Rod returned, turning her stomach. If nothing else, her ex provided a great visual reminder of mistakes she'd not repeat.

"Let's talk suspects." She reengaged Cameron's attention to the case. "Could someone involved in Quigley's original crimes be seeking revenge by coming after you?" Gracie asked, typing away to avoid looking at him.

The fresh scents of soap and a light cologne wafted to her, filling her senses.

He sat quiet for several seconds, activating her curiosity, and she glanced up. Cameron was gazing out the window, apparently caught up in his own thoughts.

"Cam?"

He blinked. "Anything is possible, but again, why now?"

"For now, let's just aim at collecting possible suspects," Gracie replied. "Then we'll weed them out with pertinent details."

"We're brainstorming people who want me dead?" Cameron deadpanned.

"Precisely."

He grunted, leaning back in his chair. "Most of the politician's staff scattered when he was brought up on charges. Anyone involved in politics knows the hazards of being connected to something negative with the potential to taint their own reputations."

"Hmm, that's true," Gracie replied. "His campaign manager would distance himself if possible?"

Cameron shrugged. "Who knows?"

"Surely, there's those devoted people who wouldn't give up on him?"

"Close friends and relatives come to mind."

"Let's start there." Gracie pulled up social media posts and old newspaper articles with pictures, then turned the screen to face Cameron. "Here are old pictures of Quigley at his political events. Does anyone stand out?"

Cameron studied the images for several long seconds. "I've spent enough time looking at the man who stole my life from me."

"I can't imagine." Gracie touched his hand, then quickly withdrew. What was she doing? "If possible, look at the pictures with an investigator eye. As in, who has motive?"

"Here's the funny thing." Cameron focused on the screen, slowly scrolling with the mouse. "Twelve years ago, I might've felt fury toward Quigley for his crimes against my family."

"You don't anymore?" Gracie asked, confused.

"Nope. I've got nothing but pity for the man. His son, Phillip—" Cameron pointed to a husky man resembling a younger version of Quigley. His light brown hair was swept stylishly to the side, and he had neatly trimmed beard. "The second man standing beside Quigley is his campaign manager, Barry Noonan." Noonan's dark beady eyes and the hint of a mustache as if he was unwilling to commit to shaving or growing one out, gave him a sinister appearance. Like a cartoon villain. He was slight not like the man who'd attacked them the night before.

"What about the woman in the picture?" Gracie asked.

Cameron nodded. "Imogene Yarborough. She was Quigley's girlfriend and glued to his side through the entire ordeal."

A woman didn't fit the profile of the male attacker, but she could've easily hired a hit man. "Hmm, did she ever threaten you?"

"Not directly, but threats were made. Your office traced everything so you'd have more access than I would."

Gracie made a note to follow up on the lead and contact SDUSM Brafford for information.

"I suppose Imogene could've orchestrated them."

"Anyone else?"

"No." Cameron shoved back from the table and gathered his plate. "Talking about Quigley eliminates my appetite."

Gracie cringed. "Sorry, I should've waited until after we'd eaten. I'll do some checking into our three suspects' current lives."

"Phillip was just a kid, the same age as me when his dad killed my parents. He missed out on all the same things I did."

Gracie swiveled to face him. "Your compassion for him surprises me."

"I wouldn't call it that." Cameron looked down.

Gracie followed his gaze to where Bane was lying, sprawled out on one side, all four paws stretched long. Not a care in the world. She envied her dog. "All right, next I'm making a list of our knowns."

"Like what?"

"The assailant wore a ski mask and gloves, long-sleeved shirt and jeans. He's a large man, but I wouldn't describe him as muscular."

Cameron nodded. "I only caught a glimpse, but I'm pretty sure he had brown eyes."

She entered the details on the form, then pulled up the pictures of Noonan and Phillip, zooming closer on their eyes. "Look at these. Do they seem familiar to the guy who attacked us yesterday?"

Cameron tugged the computer closer and stared at the images. "It all happened fast. Hard to say."

"Close your eyes and focus on the memory."

He did as she asked. "Push aside everything. Don't force yourself to make one of these fit. This is only a starting place."

"Sorry. I have nothing."

"He took off the ski mask as we were running, so I didn't see much," Gracie admitted. "At least not close enough to make a description."

"I haven't seen Phillip or Noonan, or Imogene for that matter, since I was eighteen years old. I'm sure they've changed, as have I."

"I'll do full background searches on them."

"Quigley's actions stole from his family and mine."

Gracie agreed, her mind whirling with possibilities. "What if it took the attacker this long to find you under your new identity?"

"If that's true, we have a much bigger problem."

"If they found you, so could anyone else."

"Exactly. Which reverts to my distrust of the marshals. Your office is the only one with knowledge of my identity and whereabouts."

Gracie exhaled a long breath.

"I'm not trying to be difficult. I'm not unappreciative for all the marshals have done over the years. Until now, nobody has ever gotten this close to me. If we're brainstorming suspects, it's only fair to consider the possibility your office has a leak in the WITSEC system, or a mole willing to sell me out. Quigley has money."

Gracie gathered the dishes, placing them in the sink.

Cameron joined her and leaned against the counter. "And not just me. What if there are others, too?"

Gracie scrubbed a plate, hating his logic and unable to argue against it. "I've also thought about that."

"Then we'll lay out every possibility."

"There's also the shooter," Gracie said, rinsing a plate and handing it to him to dry. "Unless they're one and the same?"

"Hmm. It's feasible there's a connection."

"As the saying goes, when you hear hooves—"

"Don't think zebras," Cameron concluded.

"Correct. He's gone to a lot of trouble to find and kill you."

Cameron dried the egg pan. "I've spent more than a decade hiding from Quigley and his associates."

"It seems to me Phillip, Imogene and Noonan have motives if they assume you ruined their lives."

"Maybe, but I don't see it." Cameron snorted. "If you're right, wouldn't that be ironic, considering Quigley destroyed my life first?"

"Revenge is a strange motive, and it fuels a lot of crimes," Gracie said.

"Quigley's assets were tied up in the campaign. He put up everything because of his arrogance, fully believing he'd win."

"What about Imogene?"

"She and Phillip were the closest family to Quigley. She wasn't married to him, so she skated on the criminal charges. Phillip was a kid, so he wasn't implicated."

"Quigley's reputation prior to the conviction paved a smooth path for both of them."

"Yep, except it's a double-edged sword because it also destroyed their future," Cameron said.

"Interesting."

They finished the dishes and returned to Gracie's computer. "Let's look at Noonan and the campaign assistant."

"Upton Shaw," Cameron provided.

Gracie pulled up the social media information.

Cameron shook his head. "Shaw is not a match. He's wiry and shorter than Noonan. Besides, he's got blue eyes, and he was older back then. The guy couldn't have possibly been the one who attacked us."

"He also passed away two years ago," Gracie said, reading the latest update on Shaw. "What about Noonan?" She pushed the screen closer.

"Hmm. Noonan has a similar build and facial features as Phillip. I hate this, but I'm second-guessing myself. Maybe the guy didn't have brown eyes?"

"Quigley's people have the most connection to you. But you also mentioned your employees and Delilah. I want to pull information on them, as well." Gracie continued typing, locating an article on Noonan. In the photo, she spotted Phillip in the background. "Noonan and Phillip were both recently in South Dakota. Looks like Noonan is working on a real estate promotional campaign."

"He'll never work in politics again." Cameron shook his head. "The guy was so tied up in Quigley's crimes, he couldn't untangle himself if he'd tried."

"Which goes to motive." Gracie met his gaze. "Cameron, I need to call my office to arrange for another marshal to join us on the case."

"You have someone on the way already."

"He's part of the DGTF and not a marshal."

"No way." Cameron got to his feet. "I don't trust anyone."

The words stung Gracie to the core. Hadn't she established trust with Cameron?

"Just tell your office you connected with me, making your welfare check. That's all they sent you here to do, right?"

She pursed her lips. "Cameron, my job is to help you, and I can't do that by hiding any part of your case."

"And if you tell your office what's going on, will they send in the calvary?"

"I don't know about that, but I should request US marshal backup."

"Negative. I'm not sticking around for that. Figure out another way."

"I can't lie to them or withhold the information." Gracie met his look with an unwavering stare. She wouldn't risk her career for his paranoia. Yet, she feared if she pushed too hard, he'd take off and become a witness on the run, which only complicated matters.

Cameron paced then exhaled a long sigh. "Look, I didn't mean to come off so harsh. I've seen you in action. I do trust you, but, Gracie, you can't guarantee other marshals aren't on the take. Who knows if Quigley had money stashed to pay an assassin. Or if Noonan is coming after me for revenge."

Gracie glanced down. "I want to argue with you because your cynicism is unhealthy." Cameron opened his mouth, but she lifted a hand. "Please, let me finish. As much as I don't agree with your skepticism, I understand your distrust. However, you're putting me in an awkward position. I have full confidence in my boss and my team. I'm obligated to keep them in the loop. But I will let them know your concerns and request to keep your status on the down-low until we've got confirmation one way or the other."

Cameron grunted. "I guess I'll have to accept that. What do you know about the new marshal they've assigned to me?"

Gracie considered the question. She didn't want to add to Cameron's already skeptical thought process, but she wouldn't lie to him, either. "I have no information on him."

Cameron's eyes widened. "Great."

"Regardless, Cam, in the end, the only trustworthy one is God. Are you a praying man?"

Cameron snorted. "Give me a break. You're a law-enforcement officer. Despite all you've endured in your personal life—your sister witnessing a murder as a child and your family's deaths—you still believe prayer is real? You can't be that naive."

"I wouldn't classify faith as naivety. My family's role in testifying to the crime Leigh witnessed changed the course of my life, and subsequently, led me to my dream career. And, yes, I've seen atrocities I'd never wish on another human being."

"Shouldn't God have stopped all that from happening?"

"Bad things happen to good people, Cam," Gracie said softly. "Sometimes because of their own actions, or the actions of another. We can't explain everything with one pat answer."

"With all you've encountered, isn't it enough to prove you can't depend on anyone but yourself? What good is prayer if God allows pain, anyway?"

Gracie glanced down, remembering the many nights she'd cried out to God about the unfairness of it all. "A normal response is a crisis of faith. We question what we believe and why. I was doing well until my family died, but I had someone special in my life."

Cameron's expression softened. "I'm sorry."

"Me, too. Anyway, it made me realize I'd misplaced my trust. My faith is what sustained and helped me to walk through that pain. In fact, each broken piece of my life somehow strengthened me." She paused. Had it? Or had she hidden behind her job? A twinge of doubt filtered through her. No healing took time. It was a process.

Where was she on that path? The marshals provided her the stability she needed, but Gracie wanted something more that included a family of her own. She was ready to move on beyond the brokenness and love again.

"Continue?" Cameron probed.

"It's like when I'm working out. I tear down the muscle and rebuild it. I tore down the places where my life was built on a flimsy foundation and rebuilt them with faith in God. I wish you could have that peace and assurance."

He frowned and Gracie recognized when to stop. Cameron had to work through his own issues, and she wouldn't push him. She also wouldn't compromise her beliefs, especially when she recognized someone hurting. Pointing them back to God was her first resort. However, she tended to be too passionate at times, and her mother's voice lingered, reminding her that faith was a personal decision, not something one forced on another.

"Some of us will never know peace," Cameron snapped. "We're destined to live always looking over one shoulder."

He stormed from the room, leaving Gracie and Bane alone.

SIX

Cameron entered the stables, battling guilt for walking out on Gracie. He also hadn't offered where he was going, though he had no doubt she was watching him through the window.

The last thing he wanted was her preaching to him about faith. He and God hadn't been on speaking terms since his parents' murder.

He never leaves you. His mother's voice lingered in the back of his mind, adding to the weight. "Yes, He did," Cameron grumbled aloud. "He left me totally alone."

Or maybe Cameron had walked away from God, but it wasn't unwarranted. God let him down when he needed the Almighty the most.

He shoved aside the stable door, inhaling the familiar smell of hay mixed with the horses' earthy scent. They whinnied at his entrance, welcoming him. Cloaked in sorrow, he strolled to the tack room and scooped their feed into a bucket.

Cameron had discarded everything at a moment's notice many times before. But for two solid years, he'd enjoyed this place, and almost felt like a normal human. Now, he'd be forced to flee and hide again. When would it end?

There was a quick rap on the door before it opened, and Gracie entered. Cameron stifled a groan.

"You can't just disappear like that," she said.

He took off his work gloves and faced her. Bane stood beside her, curiosity written in his canine expression. Cameron snagged a few treats, handing several to Gracie. "The horses love these," he replied, ignoring her comment.

Gracie turned the treat over in her hand. "Bane's never been around horses before, so he's intrigued."

The dog stood outside Sugar's gate, tilting his head from left to right. The horse ate, unphased by her audience.

"Keep an eye on him. Wouldn't want him to get stomped on accidentally." Cameron knew he wasn't being fair to Gracie, but he had two options—stay aloof, or confess his sadness of being torn from his ranch again.

She inched closer to him, peering through the door. "I have knowledge of dog breeds, but not much about horses."

"They're Arabians."

"Do you enjoy riding?" She pointed to the saddles hanging on the racks opposite them.

"I realize you're forced to babysit me, but I wouldn't mind a little alone time to think," Cameron snapped.

The hurt on Gracie's face pierced his heart.

"I'm sorry. That was uncalled for. I just… This place means a lot to me," he confessed.

Gracie nodded, compassion swarming her green irises. "Let's work together to find who is terrorizing you and get your life back to normal." She winced as though comprehending her words.

"Is that even possible?"

She remained silent for several seconds. "If your identity is compromised, probably not."

He appreciated her honesty, but it didn't reduce the pain.

"Time is of the essence," Gracie said, then quickly added, "I suppose that goes without saying."

"Yeah." Cameron grabbed a brush and started on Sugar's hide.

"Tell me about Arlee Gross."

"You're wasting your time on him. He'd never hurt me. I mean, the guy was upset, understandably so when I fired him, but…" Cameron paused, recalling Arlee had served time when he was younger. That wouldn't bode well in the man's favor with Gracie. "All right, full disclosure, although for the record, I wasn't withholding. I just remembered this information." Great, that didn't make him sound like he was trying to hide anything. Ugh.

"Okay," Gracie replied.

"Arlee was forthcoming when I hired him, but after checking into his background, I wasn't concerned." And now he sounded like he was making excuses for the man. "When Arlee was eighteen, he got involved with the wrong crowd. He was arrested and convicted of assault during a carjacking gone wrong."

"As if there are carjackings that go right?" Gracie asked, stone-faced.

"You know what I mean. They were kids and took the whole thing too far. The guy fought back."

Gracie tilted her head to the side, her expression softening. "People make mistakes."

"Precisely. Everyone I've ever met could say they regret something in their past."

Gracie didn't appear convinced. "But in the context of facts, Arlee's history conveys his potential to be violent when he wants something that he's denied or feels entitled to."

"I can't dispute that, but I never saw him exhibit criminal or violent behavior the entire time he worked for me."

"You said he was upset when you had to let him go."

"No more than anyone else would be at the loss of their only source of income." Frustrated, Cameron resumed brushing the horse. "Arlee was angry and said things he shouldn't have. Once he calmed down, he apologized. He knew he'd messed up on a few projects and owned his mistakes. I've got strong instincts and all of them say Arlee isn't involved in this."

"Well, that speaks to his maturity." Gracie crossed her arms over her chest and leaned against the stable wall. "I still think Delilah fits the suspect mold."

Cameron couldn't argue though he groaned inwardly, regretting ever mentioning the woman to Gracie. She was like a dog with a new-suspect bone. All that his short interactions with Delilah proved was his incompetence in reading people and inexperience with women. "Like I said, we met in town at the coffee shop and went out a couple of times. I'm not that intriguing."

"Again, it's her reality we're assessing, not yours."

Cameron considered her words. He'd assumed a man was out to kill him. Was Gracie right? Had Delilah planned the attacks? "Well then there's more to tell you about her."

"Okay."

"Joel said Delilah also invaded his buddy's house, leaving gifts, then threatening women he dated after they'd broken up."

"Why didn't you mention that earlier?"

Because it's humiliating to admit you didn't see the red flags. He shrugged.

"That's not normal behavior, Cam."

The dig reminded him how inexperienced he was and added to his defensiveness.

"What items did she leave for you?"

"She did that from the beginning. Little cards or treats. Harmless trinkets." Gracie's earlier warning about women's crimes of passion lingered. "Delilah did act strangely the last time I saw her."

"Elaborate, please."

"She asked questions regarding topics or people she'd have no knowledge of unless she was…following my life."

"That's stalking."

Cameron couldn't prove she'd been the one to leave the gift card for the hardware store and a picture of a cabin-restoration project. Any of his employees could've mentioned that in passing.

"You're too kind to be strict with her," Gracie said. "More men should be as thoughtful as you." She placed a hand on his shoulder.

The single touch sent his heart into an arrhythmia. He flicked a glance at her, struck by the gentleness in her eyes. He saw no condemnation or judgment. Only a tenderness that caused emotion to rise in his throat.

"Relationships are hard. There's no easy way to navigate another human being."

No, but experience makes others less foolish than me. "I didn't want to hurt her feelings. She's never been mean to me. I'm just not interested. Not that I could be if I wanted to." The bitterness returned and Cameron embraced it. The single line of defense reminded him to keep his distance from all women. Especially Gracie Fitzgerald.

"What's Delilah's last name?"

"Harris."

An engine rumbled outside. "Go ahead, I promise I'll stay right here with the horses." Relieved for a break from Gracie's interrogations, he hoped she'd take the hint.

"Let me check who it is." Gracie withdrew her gun and started for the stable door, peering out. She paused. "It's the game-and-parks officer. I'll show them where the snake traps are."

Cameron nodded, recognizing she was giving him the alone time he'd asked for. He wondered when the officer she'd requested would arrive. He dreaded dealing with another cop, but a third party might prove beneficial. Spending time with Gracie invaded Cameron's defenses, and he couldn't afford to show any gaps in his heart armor.

Not now.

Not ever.

Gracie returned to Cameron's cabin with Bane. She'd pushed him as far as she dared in their discussion. Delilah's emotional instability added to Gracie's suspicions that she could be behind the attacks. Still, it didn't explain how, if or why the woman knew Cameron's real identity.

She carried her laptop to the armchair near the window facing the entrance, where Cameron and the ranger stood outside conversing. The position allowed her to keep them in her line of sight.

Her cell phone rang. Dallas Brafford's contact information appeared on the screen. "Fitzgerald," she answered.

"Any updates?"

"Actually, quite a few." Gracie provided a synopsis of the last twenty-four hours.

"Gracie, I appreciate your willingness to assist Cameron. If I'd known this was happening, I would've made other arrangements."

"I don't mind."

"Well, you might when you hear that his assigned handler is out of town on a family emergency."

"Oh, I'm sorry to hear that." Gracie considered Cameron's request to know who his new handler would be. "Sir, may I ask who will assume Cameron's case?"

"Ormand Engel. He'll make contact with Cameron ASAP."

She'd never heard of the guy. A twinge of concern filtered through her. "Hm. I don't think I know him. No rush. Another DGTF member is coming to assist me while we work on our current case. We've got it covered." Did she sound too eager?

"I appreciate it. I'll send in a standby DUSM to cover Cameron until Ormand returns."

Brafford would replace her. She should be relieved but the idea of leaving Cameron without identifying and apprehending the attacker seemed...wrong. Or was her heart getting in the way of her common sense? She shouldn't feel this way. Hadn't Rod taught her that? Yet, disappointment at the offer had Gracie evaluating her next words carefully. "Sir, Cameron is convinced there is a leak in our system and a mole compromised his identity. He refrained from reporting into the office because of his distrust issues."

A long pause hung between them, and Gracie feared she'd overstepped her boundaries.

"I see. If that's true, and I can't guarantee it's not, then I'd say that's a huge problem."

"Absolutely."

"The WITSEC program has a solid history. Any breach of information poses huge risks to many witnesses. I've not heard of any other issues. Most importantly, I struggle to view any of my people as disloyal."

"I'm inclined to agree. However, for the time being, I respectfully request approval to stay with Cameron. I've established a foundation of trust with him during our encounters with the assailant. I'll handle his protection detail while working on the taskforce case."

"That's stretching you thin."

"Not a problem. Plus, it sounds like Ormand has a lot going on," Gracie replied. "I want to help Cameron. Besides, after the shootout and the snake in front of my cabin, threatening mine and Bane's lives, things got personal."

"Can't dispute that," Brafford replied. "I'll approve it for now, but I won't take a witness's word over my loyal employees. We'll revisit this discussion in forty-eight hours. If there's been no progress, I'll consider alternative plans."

In other words, he would bring out the big guns and dismiss her. She had to help Cameron, and fast.

They disconnected. She'd bought a window of time, but eventually, he'd have to come to terms with establishing a working relationship with his new handler if he wanted WITSEC protection. They couldn't force him to remain in the program, and with the breach in his identity, she almost didn't blame him if he refused.

Gracie called Daniel to update him on the situation.

"That's seriously concerning," her team leader replied.

"Yeah, whoever is after Cameron is tenacious."

"And they apparently have no problem taking collateral damage in their hunt," Daniel said. "I'm sorry Zach is delayed. Now more than ever, I want to make sure he gets there to help you."

"I think for now the danger is minimized. Cameron is finishing up with the game-and-parks ranger, and we're staying on high alert," Gracie explained. "In the meantime, I'm researching possible suspects who have motive, opportunity and means to hurt Cameron."

"I'll notify the team," Daniel said. "Keep us updated."

Gracie pocketed her phone. Cameron and the ranger stood talking easily. She debated joining them and decided against it. Cameron needed space and he was within her visual.

She opened her laptop. She'd dig as much as she could while waiting for Zach then ask for Cheyenne's help to conduct research into Phillip

Quigley, the senator's son, and Barry Noonan, the former campaign manager. Based on the most recent social media updates online, Noonan maintained gainful employment. He'd taken a hit in his career trajectory, descending from powerhouse Walter Quigley's go-to man to working as a social media officer for a startup company. Still, the man seemed to have the gift of gab, if you bought in to his sales pitches. Gracie watched the most recent video showing Noonan at his current employer's kickoff event. The company's solicitation for funds to speed up the development of their biggest project to date—improvement of older crime-ridden areas with the vision of bringing the neighborhoods to luxury status—was motivating. Gracie had seen similar ventures that renovated dying downtown communities into expensive lofts and condominium housing.

She leaned back against the cushion. If Noonan was involved in the attacks on Cameron, why now? None of it made sense. Pronghorn Hills Guest Ranch was located far from the largest cities in South Dakota, in the middle of nowhere, near Badlands National Park. There weren't older neighborhoods to regenerate. If anything, they would have to develop the land and that was expensive.

Noonan had no financial motive to come after Cameron now. However, revenge for ruining his career remained a feasible motive. Noonan had lost a lot, but he'd landed on his feet. She continued diving into Noonan's life and located a story where he'd admitted his aspirations of making it to the White House eventually. He'd had big dreams that were destroyed with Quigley's case.

She pulled up the recent video of Noonan again. Her skin crawled at his overzealous mannerisms and oily polished responses to the media. Barry Noonan emitted creepy vibes. The kind of guy who'd say or do anything to get what he wanted. To the untrained eye, Noonan appeared knowledgeable and accomplished, but she'd seen enough con men in her career to recognize deceit. She'd studied human behavior extensively. No amount of expensive clothes covered up someone with Noonan's lack of ethics.

He clearly possessed the ability to convince people he was worth hiring. He remained a solid suspect, but certainly not the only one. Before she requested Cheyenne's assistance, she wanted to narrow down all the possibilities.

Next, she pulled up Imogene Yarborough, who'd been the senator's girlfriend at the time of the murder. The woman came from considerable financial means, which she'd mostly maintained, other than the losses she'd incurred from supporting Quigley. However, her connection to the corrupt politician stained her social status and reputation. Yet, she'd stood faithfully beside Quigley throughout his trial, appearing in all the newspaper photos. If she'd found Cameron, a crime of passion to avenge losing her boyfriend and status wasn't out of the question. A deeper dive, however, revealed Imogene had suspiciously vanished from the social scene two years ago.

People didn't disappear, but with her financial means, Imogene had the ability to reinvent herself. Maybe she'd changed her name. Gracie made a note. Perhaps Cheyenne would uncover details about Imogene.

Next, she pulled up Phillip Quigley. He also worked in real estate development. Interesting that he'd chosen a similar career field to Noonan. Phillip was unmarried and, for the most part, he kept a low profile. Understandable, considering how his father's fall from grace had dragged their family name through the social dregs.

Both Philip and Barry had similar facial features and skin coloring, which kept them at the top of her list as possible suspects as the attacker. However, there was no way she could say either qualified with complete confidence. It was dark and she'd only glimpsed the assailant for a moment before he disappeared into the forest. The one thing that stood out was both Noonan and Phillip had visited Plains City, South Dakota, recently.

Gracie tapped her finger on the edge of the laptop. Were Philip and Noonan working together? That wasn't a stretch—in fact, it made sense since both were in real-estate development. A business partnership was feasible. Or were they competitors?

And if so, what did that have to do with Cameron?

The biggest issue was who and how someone

had discovered Cameron's real identity. Too many questions bounced around in Gracie's mind and she needed solid leads.

As if on cue, her cell phone chimed with a text message from the DGTF tech analyst, Cheyenne Chen. Heard about the recent trouble there. Is there anything I can do to help?

Though Cheyenne's responsibilities lay with the task force, her assistance on Cameron's case was like having a super power behind Gracie. Cheyenne's excellent resources would no doubt help tremendously. She typed, Your timing is impeccable. Do you have hidden cameras?

I'd never tell if I did.

Gracie grinned at the tech's quick wit. She responded: Would you dig into Phillip Quigley, Barry Noonan and Imogene Yarborough for me? Gracie considered adding in Delilah and Arlee, but preferred to do her own research on them first.

On it, Cheyenne replied.

Thank you.

Gracie contacted the local PD and requested information on Delilah Harris and Arlee Gross, which she received via email within minutes.

Several men in surrounding towns had filed complaints against Delilah for stalking, breaking and entering, and trespassing, but no charges were issued because of the lack of evidence. Delilah had refuted the complaints, claiming the men had given her keys to their place. The authorities had a he-said-she-said situation and hadn't had the ability to proceed. Interestingly, Delilah seemed to back off on the men after they'd filed complaints, which told Gracie she feared law enforcement to some degree. However, her repeated offenses were strikingly similar, which indicated she was perfecting her criminal skills.

By contrast, Arlee Gross's criminal background contained charges and a conviction dated twenty years prior. His history of violence and theft coincided with what Cameron had shared. Arlee was eighteen at the time of the incident. He'd acted foolishly and in the heat of the moment, costing him several years of his freedom. However, he'd not acted out criminally since. Perhaps Cameron's instincts about the man were accurate, and Arlee had learned his lesson early on.

Regardless, she remained suspicious of the two. Delilah could've hired the assailant, maybe even hired Arlee to attack them. His mug shot revealed dark hair and eyes, both similar features to Noonan and Phillip. When she'd dug as far as she could on her own, Gracie texted Cheyenne, requesting assistance on Arlee and Delilah. If Delilah was as skilled as it sounded in manipulating men to do what she wanted, it was possible she'd convinced Arlee to go after Cameron for revenge. For both of them.

The sound of an engine captured her attention and Gracie spotted the game-and-parks ranger's truck exiting the premises. Her gaze roved the area, searching for Cameron.

She pushed back from the table and walked to the window to gain a better look.

Gracie rushed to the door, Bane at her side immediately. She bolted outside, pausing to check the porch for reptiles before stepping onto the ground. "Cameron?"

Silence.

She scanned the landscape. Panic rose in her chest as the ranger's truck disappeared over the hill.

Where had he gone?

SEVEN

"Cameron!"

He dropped the horse's brush and sprinted out of the stables at the panic in Gracie's voice. He rounded the building, nearly colliding with her.

"What's wrong?" Cameron skidded to a halt.

"Where were you?" He reared back at Gracie's harsh reprimand. "I'm sorry, I just… I want to make sure you're safe." Concern etched her forehead, dissipating his irritation.

"I saw you through my cabin window, working on your computer, and figured I'd finish brushing Rocket," he explained.

"Oh, thanks." She smiled.

The approach of a vehicle interrupted them, and Cameron turned, spotting the Keystone sheriff's patrol unit pulling through the gated entrance. "I asked the ranger to close the gate when he left. Guess I should've waited and done it myself," he grumbled, then quipped, "Not that it keeps the killer from getting to us."

"That's Deputy Zach Kelcey," Gracie said.

Cameron grunted. How had he gone from a

peaceful existence to having not one but two law-enforcement officers invading his space?

Gracie moved toward the unit, gesturing for the deputy to park outside Cameron's cabin. He watched as a tall man exited the vehicle, releasing a black Labrador. The dogs exchanged customary sniffs, tails wagging in approval. Gracie and the deputy spoke, and Cameron spotted the curious glance they aimed in his direction. He inhaled a fortifying breath and approached.

"Zach, meet Cameron Holmes," Gracie said, introducing the men. "Like Bane and I, Amber and Zach were also recruited by the Dakota Gun Task Force."

The task force was probably throwing resources in to try and get Gracie back faster since Cameron wasn't her assignment.

"Mr. Holmes," the deputy said, extending a hand.

"Call me Cameron."

"Zach Kelcey. And this is Amber." He gestured toward the Labrador. "Gracie was catching me up on the last twenty-four hours. Sounds like you two had quite the adventure."

Cameron grunted, shoving his hands into his pockets. "That's one way to describe it."

"I can't believe this creep seriously left rattlesnakes for you." Zach shook his head. "That takes premeditation to a whole new level."

"Tell me about it."

"Cameron was a genius, though," Gracie replied. "He handled the reptiles like a pro using some kind of special prong. He secured them into a trap, remaining totally calm. I could barely breathe watching him."

Zach's gaze bounced between Gracie and Cameron. Cameron's neck warmed again under her appraisal. *Knock it off. She's trying to stay in your trust zone with compliments. Keep yourself guarded.* Yet for all his self-talk, Cameron couldn't help but appreciate Gracie's thoughtfulness.

"Our tech specialist is working on the list of suspects Cameron and I compiled earlier today," Gracie explained. "All have motives and hopefully Cheyenne's search reveals more."

Cameron doubted that, but he didn't argue. He also did a doubletake. She'd involved another task force person?

"I read your case file," Zach said, addressing Cameron. "Based on what Gracie told me with the extended timeframe, Quigley's connections don't fit."

"That's what I said," Cameron agreed. Maybe this guy wasn't so bad. "For them to come after me after all these years makes no sense. There's no way they'd know I live out here."

"Unless there's a mole or a leak in the WITSEC system," Zach concluded.

"Cameron said the same thing," Gracie replied. "For obvious reasons, I struggle to believe that's true. I believe in the system, otherwise why work for it?"

"But it's not out of the question."

Cameron liked Zach more by the minute. He understood Gracie's obligation to defend her office, but he appreciated Zach's willingness to look beyond the law-enforcement brotherhood.

"While we wait to hear back from Cheyenne, we need to work on the DGTF case," Zach said. "Daniel wants us to finish those interviews."

"I'll be fine here while you two do that." Hope returned at the possibility of time alone.

Gracie and Zach exchanged a look.

Or not. "What?" Cameron asked.

"Cameron, we'd prefer if you stayed with us," Gracie said.

"Um, no." Cameron shook his head. "I've got tons to finish around here." Though his efforts might prove futile if WITSEC forced him to move. And for the first time since the whole Quigley incident occurred, Cameron considered refusing their protection. After all, he was supposed to be under their care and was currently dodging a killer. They were failing.

"Negative," Zach said. "But I empathize with you. Tell you what, we'll come back and help you around here to make up for the time we're absconding from your schedule."

"I can't report to my boss that I left a witness," Gracie explained.

Cameron shot them a skeptical glance but relented with a shrug. "Fine. But the animals can't wait. I'll finish their care before we leave."

"What can we do?" Zach asked.

"They need water if you want to refill the trough." Cameron gestured toward the large steel bin. "Hose is on the outside of the stables."

"Absolutely," Zach said, rounding the building with the dogs trailing him.

Cameron entered the stables with Gracie beside him. "Thank you for agreeing to join us while we conduct our interviews for the gun-trafficking case I told you about earlier."

"I don't think it's necessary, I can take care of myself," Cameron argued.

"I apologize for dragging you away from your place, but I'm hoping it won't take long," Gracie said.

Cameron opened the stall doors and let Rocket and Sugar outside. They strolled to the bale of hay centered in their pen.

"They know exactly what to do," she said.

"This is our routine."

"Hmm." Gracie paused, facing him. "Routines make it easy for whoever is after you to keep your schedule, too."

Cameron measured her words. "Probably not a bad thing that we leave for a while today."

Gracie glanced at the horses. "Do you allow your guests to ride?"

"Yes, it's an add-on option. I discontinued the trail rides to stick close to the ranch when I worried someone was watching me," Cameron said. "I didn't want to leave the grounds unattended."

Zach returned. "The horses are beautiful."

Cameron smiled. “Growing up in Wyoming, we had horses,” he explained more to Zach than to Gracie, since they’d already discussed the topic. “Something about them recharges me.”

“Is this place a lot of work for you?” Zach asked.

“Yes,” Cameron said. “But it’s a labor of love as corny as that sounds.”

“Not at all,” Gracie replied. “My dad used to say if you do something you love, you never work a day in your life.”

“I would agree except I love hard work.” Cameron sighed. Pointless efforts he’d made that the government would strip from his hands without recompense. He shook off the thought. “How can I help with the interviews you need to conduct?”

“Just need a place to develop our POA,” Zach replied.

Cameron recognized the reference to a point-of-action plan. “Meet at my cabin.”

“I’ll grab my bag and meet you there,” Zach said, hurrying ahead of them.

Cameron leaned against the split-rail fence. “I hate that my life is a moving target. This place provides peace like I’ve never known before. I finally found a way to grow roots and invest in my future. I’ve worked hard to make this ranch a business and a home. All of it was going well for once. Now, I’m wary, looking over my shoulder. That gets old fast.”

Gracie nodded and turned. He followed her gaze, viewing the beautiful acreage with the four strategically positioned guest cabins—purposefully situated to provide privacy for the residents, while maintaining a community environment. His luxe cabin stood closest to the entrance.

Wordlessly, they made their way to his cabin, where Zach waited on the porch. Bane and Amber sniffed the exterior grounds, staying close. Gracie and Zach set up at the dining table. Cameron leaned against the kitchen counter, within eavesdropping proximity, while staying out of their way.

Both faced Gracie's laptop and he inched closer, spotting the live video. "Hey, Cheyenne," Zach said.

"We're prepping for the trip to interview Petey Pawners's family and associates," Gracie explained. "Any change or updates we need to consider?"

"Petey's mother owns a hair salon in the next town," Cheyenne replied. "I'll send you the address."

"Thanks," Gracie said.

They disconnected, and seconds later, lifted their phones. "Let's start with his mother and work our way back here," Zach suggested.

"Cameron can ride with me," Gracie said, "and we'll follow you."

"Sounds good." Zach led the way, K-9 Amber trotting happily beside him.

Cameron locked up his cabin and followed Gracie to her vehicle. He climbed into the passenger seat while Gracie loaded K-9 Bane into his kennel. Cameron studied the vehicle, where a slider door separated him from the front seats while permitting him to also interact with them. Gracie closed the slider. "He loves to be part of the conversation, but has issues with personal space," she chuckled.

"I don't mind," Cameron said.

Gracie started the engine and snapped on her seat belt. "I'm down with helping to work on the cabins, with the disclaimer that I'm clueless about construction, and I can't vouch for Zach's experience either."

Cameron snickered. "Willingness is half the battle."

The vehicles exited the ranch and Gracie parked, waiting for Cameron to close and lock the gate. He peered out at his home, hoping he wouldn't return to ruins. Surely, the assassin's goal was killing Cameron. Not destroying his property.

But a chill slithered up his spine at the recollection of the snakes. He slid into the passenger seat for the second time, snapping on his seat belt, his eyes glued on the side mirror as the ranch slowly faded from sight.

Gracie's failed attempts to engage Cameron in conversation resulted in clipped replies. No doubt, he feared for his ranch and the horses. Rightly so. She prayed the attacker wouldn't bother either, but offering Cameron platitudes would fall flat. She opted for silence instead. Truthfully, her motives weren't altruistic. Gracie had her own closet-skeletons to deal with as she returned to Black Hawk.

She tried ignoring the urge to reminisce, but the site of the Old Towne Creamery took her breath away. Leigh loved that place and always ordered the same strawberry ice cream with chocolate chips in a waffle cone.

Gracie never ate strawberry ice cream anymore for that reason.

By the time she pulled into the space beside Zach's patrol unit, Gracie desperately needed to shift into marshal mode and divert her thoughts into work talk. "Guess this is the place." *You're a brilliant conversationalist, Gracie.*

A colorful sign that read *Patsy's Beauty Parlor* hung over the storefront door. She parked and faced Cameron. "I'll leave Bane with you. We might stress out Patsy if she sees us with two K-9s in tow." The comment was mostly true. She also wanted to ensure Cameron's protection and Bane was the best alternative.

"Sure." His reply told her he wasn't buying the excuse, but he didn't argue.

"We'll be right back."

Zach had already exited his vehicle and stood waiting with K-9 Amber.

With one last glance over her shoulder, Gracie and Zach entered the salon. The blaring of hair dryers, loud upbeat music and the strong scent of ammonia filled the air. Another stylist with wild red ponytails on either side of her head stood wrapping an older woman's hair in tight permanent curlers, which explained the smell.

A woman sat at the reception desk, typing into the computer. "Welcome to Patsy's. How can I help you?" She glanced up, her smile fading at the sight of Gracie, Zach and Amber.

The woman, in her late forties, had her dark hair styled in loose curls around her face, giving her a younger appearance. She wore a bright sundress with splatters of yellow, orange and pink flowers.

"Hi there," Gracie said. "We're looking for Patsy Pawners."

"Why?" She quirked a perfectly trimmed eyebrow.

"Just need to talk with her," Zach replied.

"Congratulations, you found her." Patsy leaned back in her seat, a challenge written in her expression.

The other stylist paused in her discussion with her client, flicking a curious glance their direction.

"Could we speak privately?" Gracie asked, lowering her voice.

"Sure." Patsy stood and ushered them toward a room at the back. Fingernail polishes and manicure supplies were centered on the clear plastic table. They took seats opposite Patsy. "I can't imagine why you need to talk to me."

Gracie folded her hands on the table. "First, you have our condolences for your son, Petey."

The woman nodded, but her lip quivered slightly. "Is that what this is about?"

"Yes," Zach said. "We have questions about your son's activities and acquaintances."

A conflicted expression passed over her face before she replied, "What's there to say? He's gone."

Gracie caught the sorrow in the woman's tone, and her heart squeezed. No matter what Petey had done, Patsy was a grieving mother who had lost her child. "Mrs. Pawners—"

"Patsy," she corrected. "My mother-in-law is Mrs. Pawners and there's not a meaner woman on the planet."

"Patsy, do you have any idea who'd want to hurt Petey?"

She snorted. "As you might've guessed, my son and I weren't especially close." Patsy met her gaze, a steeliness filling her eyes. "He hung out with the dregs of society. Could've been a hundred different people. Petey had a way of befriending the biggest losers in the world. I told him a million times to stay away from them, but he was drawn to trouble like a bee to honey." Her tone tensed and a flash of anger passed over her face.

Though Gracie wasn't sure who the emotion was aimed at, it was evident they'd hit a nerve with the question.

"Honestly, I've expected this visit and conversation for years. He loved living on the edge. I warned Petey his foolish ways would catch up with him. Told him time and again he'd pay for all he'd done. But just like his daddy, he wouldn't listen to me." She lifted her chin. "I braced myself for years, preparing for that moment when I'd learn my boy was gone. Guess that day has come."

Zach and Gracie exchanged a glance. Though Patsy's tone was irate, her pain shown through.

They needed to regroup. As though sensing the invitation, Amber moved closer, pinning Patsy with a compassionate gaze.

"What's your dog do?" Patsy asked.

The canines were always a good ice-breaker and tension reliever.

"This is K-9 Amber," Zach said. "She's trained in search-and-rescue."

Patsy's demeanor softened. "May I pet her?"

"Yes." Zach addressed Amber. "Go ahead."

The dog inched over to Patsy, accepting the gentle strokes. "Hey, pretty girl."

After several seconds, Zach leaned forward, elbows resting on his knees. "Patsy, can you remember the names of anyone Petey hung around with? We really could use your help to find a lead on his killer."

Patsy lifted her head as if suddenly remembering they were in the room. With a final glance at Amber, she pushed back from the table and stood. "No. I'd love to help you, but I can't."

Can't or won't? Gracie shot Zach the question in her eyes.

"Well, thank you for your time," Zach said, getting to his feet.

"Yes, and again our condolences for your loss." Gracie trailed Zach and Amber out of the building.

Gracie looked at Cameron, apparently deep in discussion with Bane, who panted softly beside him. She grinned. "Glad those two are bonding."

"I appreciate a dog lover." Zach withdrew his

phone. "Looks like Cheyenne sent us a few more names."

Gracie pulled out her cell phone and stared at the list. "It's a long shot, but how about we aim for Grandma Pawners?"

Zach chuckled. "Well, if she's as mean as Patsy said, I'm scared."

"I'll protect you," Gracie joked.

They separated and climbed into their respective vehicles, Zach taking the lead.

"How'd it go?" Cameron asked once they were on the road again.

"Not great." Gracie jerked her chin toward him. "I saw you two getting acquainted, though."

In response, Bane nudged her with his nose.

"Yeah, he's pretty cool," Cameron said. "Where are we headed now?"

"Another of Petey's relatives."

"Is this a typical day for you?" Cameron asked.

"What?"

"Driving around with your dog, talking to people?"

"Whatever gets the job done. We're hunting down leads and that's gotta come from someone else. No matter how much people try to hide, everybody knows something about someone. We need to find that person."

Cameron grew quiet.

Gracie considered her words, wincing inwardly. Yet, she'd meant what she said and the same was true of whoever had exposed Cameron's real identity. Finding that person was essential. And fast.

Gracie and Zach drove through town and eventually pulled up to a tiny, run-down, clapboard house, parking on the street. Gracie wasn't familiar with the area.

"I'll stay with Bane," Cameron offered with an accompanying sigh, though his smile said he didn't mind.

"Thanks." Gracie exited the vehicle and joined Zach and Amber on the sidewalk.

Zach rapped twice on the metal of the broken screen door. When there was no response, he tried again, this time on the chipped paint front door.

"I'm coming. Hold your ponies!" a voice called from the other side.

The door swung wide and an older woman with a mass of white hair resembling cotton candy glowered at them. Her weathered face behind bright, red-framed glasses held no tenderness. "Whaddya want?" she barked.

Guess Patsy hadn't embellished her mother-in-law's demeanor.

"Hi there," Gracie said. "I'm Deputy US Marshal Gracie Fitzpatrick and this is Keystone Deputy Zach Kelcey."

"Yeah?" She leaned against the doorframe, clearly not intending to invite them inside. Her gaze scoured both, then moved to where Amber sat quietly beside Zach. "I hate dogs."

Gracie bristled.

"We're here regarding your grandson, Petey," Zach said, ignoring the woman's comment.

"Hmm. Well, you're a little late. Maybe you ain't heard yet, but Petey's dead."

"Yes, ma'am, we're aware," Gracie added softly. "We're sorry for your loss."

She snorted. "If you knew him, you wouldn't be. I got nothing else to say." She turned on her heel and slammed the door.

Gracie and Zach stared at each other.

"Alrighty then," Gracie said.

"Next," Zach grunted.

Gracie pulled out her phone. "We've got a cousin about twenty miles outside of here." She stifled her relief at leaving Black Hawk.

"Let's give it a whirl," Zach replied.

They met with Petey's cousin, a twiggy man jumpier than a mouse in front of twenty cats. He offered no information and claimed he hadn't seen Petey in months.

Next, they traveled to Patsy's brother and barely made it onto his front steps before he growled that they were violating his rights by interviewing him. Lastly, they tried Petey's aunt on his father's side. She slammed the door in their faces when they identified themselves.

They pulled over at a convenience store near the highway to regroup and let the dogs out for a break.

"This is getting us nowhere," Gracie grumbled.

Cameron crossed his arms over his chest. "Wish I could help you out."

"You could deputize him," Zach teased.

"Um, no thanks," Cameron chuckled. "Bane and I are getting acquainted while you two win over people."

"It's been a joy," Gracie mumbled sarcastically.

"We've got one more on the list, and it's on our way back to the ranch," Zach said.

"Good, because it'll be time for the evening chores by then," Cameron replied. "Remember, you two offered to help."

"Duly noted," Gracie chuckled.

The trio loaded up and drove to the big-box store. They parked near the loading docks, where Cheyenne had advised a guy affiliated with Petey worked. They only had his first name, but it was unusual, and they hoped to track him down quickly.

Sure enough, as Gracie approached the dock, she spotted a man, early twenties, with long, blond hair, hoisting boxes off a pallet. "Hi there."

He twisted around to face her, sweat dripping from his brow. He was wearing a T-shirt soaked with perspiration and dirty black jeans. "Hey." He paused, checking her out. "What're you doing out here, pretty lady?"

Gracie tried not to laugh at his flirtation attempt. "Got a minute?"

"Sure."

"We're looking for Hobart?" Zach said, coming around the corner.

He stood up straighter. "Oh, hey, man." Noticing Zach's uniform, he added, "Officer. Uh, yeah.

That's me." His gaze bounced between Gracie, Amber and Zach.

"We're here regarding Petey Pawners," Zach said.

Hobart's skin blanched and he swallowed hard enough to make his Adam's apple move. He glanced over his shoulder and lowered his voice. "I don't know who you're talking about."

"You're not in trouble," Gracie said. "We're investigating Petey. Not you."

Hobart blinked a couple of times. "Okay."

"What can you tell us regarding Petey's friends or others he was involved with?" Gracie asked.

Hobart swallowed again, his eyes shifting from left to right, on constant watch. "I only knew Petey through an acquaintance. We weren't buddies or nothing."

"Who was the associate?" Zach asked.

Hobart blinked, apparently regretting that he'd mentioned another person. "Can't remember his name. Dude, Petey was—" Hobart seemed to consider his next words. "He was bad news. Always hustling. Not the kind of guy you went up against."

"Why?" Gracie asked. "We need anything you can give us."

Hobart opened his mouth and his gaze traveled past them.

Gracie spotted a sedan in the distance with illegally tinted windows. "Who's that?"

"Nobody." Hobart shook his head. "I told you. You don't cross guys like Petey."

"That's not an issue. Petey's dead," Zach replied.

Gracie watched as the sedan drove away slowly. "If you're afraid of someone, we can help."

Hobart grunted. "Doubtful." He pushed back, wiping his palms on his jeans. "Did you help Petey?"

"He didn't ask for it," Zach countered.

"Whatever. How'd he die?" Hobart pinned Gracie with a stare.

She started to speak, and he cut her off. "Doesn't matter. No way. I'm not talking to you guys, or I'll be next. Talk to my lawyer." He spun on his heel and hurried inside the building.

Gracie and Zach returned to their units.

"At least we finished the day with a perfect zero," Gracie said, deadpan.

They called Daniel with a quick update. "I wish I was surprised by that news, but I'm not," he said.

"We're headed back to Cameron's ranch," Zach said.

In response to his name, Cameron peered out the passenger window, no doubt eavesdropping.

"Good. Don't worry," Daniel assured them. "I'm sure we'll get a solid lead soon. Criminals always leave a trail."

They disconnected and a revving engine gained their attention.

"Get down!" Zach hollered.

The group ducked just as rapid gunfire exploded around them. Before they could return fire, the same sedan they'd seen at the big box store sped from sight.

EIGHT

By the time they reached Pronghorn Hills Guest Ranch, Gracie was wiped out. She'd started out enjoying the interviews. That was the part of her job she liked most, but not discovering new leads had left her frustrated. All roads from Petey Pawners's acquaintances or family members were nothing more than a series of dead ends.

"Thanks again for coming along and hanging out with Bane while we conducted the interviews," Gracie said.

"It was interesting to watch. From a distance," Cameron replied. "I wasn't able to hear most of what you said, but I noticed you have a way with people."

"Really?"

"You treat them with respect while exuding your authority. You don't go in with the attitude of bullying people into giving you information."

"No, that technique never worked for me."

"Well, it's nice to see."

"Thanks, Cameron." Gracie's heart warmed at his praise. Cameron stroke Bane's head. "He's taken a liking to you. He doesn't do that with everyone, it's a huge compliment."

"I'm contemplating adopting a pet. I love the horses, but if things don't work out..." His voice trailed off and he turned away. "Anyway, animals are easy to talk to. We've only recently met, and I can't say for certain, but I'm confident he won't tell any of my secrets," Cameron joked.

"You confided in Bane?"

Cameron's face blushed. "Maybe."

Gracie laughed. "He's kept all mine, so I think you're safe with him."

She waited as Cameron hopped out and released the gate, allowing her to enter. Gracie rolled down the window. "Zach should be right behind us with the food. In the meantime, I'd like to conduct a perimeter search to ensure we're not walking into an ambush."

Cameron closed the gate and climbed into the passenger seat. "He's got the code." He remained in the vehicle, while Gracie checked the exterior of the cabins and property. And the horses roamed peacefully in their pen. When she returned, Cameron asked, "Well?"

"All clear."

Relief flooded Cameron's face. Zach pulled up with bags of food for dinner, and Cameron stowed the food in the microwave to keep it warm while Gracie gave the dogs a potty break. They'd help Cam with the evening chores and then they'd eat.

"Follow me," Cameron said, stepping onto the porch. He led them to the stables.

Gracie enjoyed the physical labor, which seemed like the wrong term. The horses brought a sense of peace, and she liked feeding and securing them in their stalls for the evening. When they'd finished, the trio returned to Cameron's cabin for dinner.

"What did you pick up for us?" Gracie asked as she poured bowls of food for the dogs, then traded places with Zach at the sink to wash her hands.

"Hamburgers and fries," Zach replied with a smile.

"Sounds good to me." Cameron removed the food from the microwave where he'd stored it. "It's a little cold."

"Cops are used to eating cold food," Gracie half joked.

"It never fails," Zach explained. "As soon as we sit down, we'll get a call and have to leave."

They settled at the table and dug into the meal.

"I rarely sit down for any meal since I normally eat alone," she admitted. And that sounded pathetic.

"Me, too," Cameron said.

She shot him a grateful glance. "I usually eat popcorn while standing by the sink."

"Chips and salsa are my go-to," Cameron said.

"Yeah, lately, I have meals on the run," Zach said.

His comment invoked her curiosity. How was Zach doing? She had limited knowledge of his personal life and the situation with his wife. Not wanting to press him for information in front of Cameron, she decided to talk to him when they were alone.

"This is a treat," Cameron said biting into a French fry. "I rarely go out to eat. It's too hard when I have guests here. I like to stick close in case they need anything."

The dogs finished their dinner and settled beside the sofa with contented sighs.

"Your ranch is incredible," Zach said. "It's plain to see why you love living here."

Gracie saw the sadness cloud Cameron's face and she empathized with him.

"I appreciate the help you provided today. It made the chores go quickly," he replied, diverting topics. It was something Gracie noticed he did often.

"We're not finished, right?" Zach asked. "Which cabin do you want us to start working on first?"

"Don't worry about it." Cameron dipped a fry in ketchup.

"Nope, we're committed," Gracie insisted.

"I'm working on cabin one's renovations at the moment."

"Count me in," Zach said. "I don't have a ton of my tools with me, but I'm happy to help."

"Tools are not a problem," Cameron replied. "Those I have in abundance."

"Zach, you're experienced in construction?" Gracie asked.

Zach shot her a feigned look of offense. "Um, yeah. I love working on projects around the house.

Used to do a lot of it. Thanks to the HGTV network and their home-renovation shows. Eden always had great ideas. She'd start out by saying 'hey, I was thinking' and I knew I was going to be working on something." Zach glanced down, averting his eyes.

The slight shift confirmed Gracie's suspicions that something was wrong at the Kelcey home.

"Who's Eden?" Cameron asked.

"My wife." Zach took a bite of his burger.

Gracie intervened to alleviate the awkwardness. "Not sure how much help I'll be, but I'm willing to try."

Cameron finished his dinner, putting his wrappers into the paper bag. "I'll grab tools at the shed and meet you guys at Cabin One."

"Sounds good," Gracie said.

She and Zach walked with the dogs trotting happily beside them. "I didn't want to ask in front of Cameron, but everything okay with Eden?"

"No," Zach said dejected. "We've been separated for a few months. I'm miserable but surviving." He shoved his hands into his pockets. "I don't really want to talk about it. No offense."

"None taken. But if you need an ear, I'm here."

"Thanks, I appreciate it."

"I'm praying you'll work it out." Gracie never told her team about Rod, and now didn't seem like the time to bring it up. After all, it wasn't like she had any experience in marriage. She hadn't even made it down the aisle. But she understood pain and loss.

Cameron joined them, carrying a toolbox, and unlocked the cabin door.

The small single room held a queen-size bed, small sofa, a fireplace and a kitchenette. Gracie noticed all the cabinets were missing doors.

"I'm refacing them. The cabinets are in good shape, but they're dated," Cameron explained. "How do you feel about sanding?" he asked Zach.

"I've done a little bit of everything," Zach said with a smile.

"Excellent." Cameron handed him the sander and showed him where he had set out each of the cabinet doors.

Zach whistled as he got to work.

Gracie faced Cameron. "What can I do?"

"Do you have any carpentry experience?"

"Nope."

He laughed. "Honesty is a great quality. I'm replacing the hardware on the sinks, shower and door handles. You could remove the old ones."

"That sounds doable." Gracie glanced around. The cabin was older and dated, not as fancy as her assigned unit. "Will you be putting in the French doors like those installed in my cabin?"

"No, this one is a simpler, budget-friendly model. But I want it to be refreshed." Cameron handed her the appropriate screwdriver and offered a quick tutorial. "Good to go?"

"Yep, I'll holler if I have issues." Gracie started removing the screws on the doorknobs.

Music filled the cabin and Gracie sang along

with the familiar song. She laughed when she heard Cameron and Zach belting out the lyrics. Gracie hurried to join them as they sang their hearts out with over emphasized air guitars and drum solos. When the song finished, they laughed.

"I needed that," Cameron said.

"I think we all did." Gracie offered a wave. "Back to work." She returned to the bathroom, finishing her assignment.

Once that was done, she moved to the sink, then walked out to the kitchen, where Cameron and Zach were chatting and laughing like old friends. It was the lightest she'd seen either man the entire time she'd known them.

"You guys are having too much fun," she said.

"But we're getting the job done," Zach countered.

Bane's sudden bark interrupted their lightheartedness.

The group turned, spotting the Malinois standing on guard. Amber sat, ears perked. Bane rushed to the door, delivering several warning barks.

In what felt like slow motion, Gracie, Cameron and Zach went silent. Gracie released her gun from the leg holster, Zach brandished his duty weapon and they rushed for the door.

The hair on her arms rose in visceral response. "Down!" She dove for the floor, tackling Bane simultaneously.

Gunshots riddled the cabin, shattering the windows. Gracie looked over her shoulder.

Cameron, Zach and Amber hid behind the couch as bullets pelted the walls and furniture.

Gracie crept to the window then flattened against the wall, searching for the shooter.

The gunfire ceased.

"Stay with Cameron! We're going after him." Gracie snapped on Bane's leash. "Bane, *zook*!"

"I'm going!" Cameron stood.

"Negative," Gracie replied. "It'll go faster with Bane and I." She and Bane exited the cabin, taking cover behind rocks and trees along the way. Bane sniffed the path, tugging against the lead. Gracie's senses were on high alert, and her pulse raged in her ears, making it hard to listen for any movement. As they entered the forest, she kept Bane's leash short, forcing him to stick close to her.

A blast sounded and a bullet pierced the tree trunk beside her. Gracie dove, yanking Bane down with her. They hid behind the tree line, and she returned fire.

Bane barked, ready to pursue the shooter.

Gracie held his leash, unwilling to risk his life by releasing him to a hidden gunman.

They continued the pursuit, chasing the shooter through the woods. She recognized the area that they'd walked through the day before. The guy had parked in the same space. A figure loomed ahead, shadowed and too far away for her to see his face. She and Bane sprinted after him, but he reached a compact sedan first, jumping into the driver's seat.

The car sped away before Gracie and Bane

reached him. "Ugh!" she cried out in frustration. Bane barked furiously.

They'd lost him.

Again.

Gracie and Bane schlepped back to the cabin to report the situation. They checked on the horses and found the stable locked and secured.

Cameron and Zach were working to fix the shattered windows temporarily for the night.

"We're going to catch him," Zach assured the group.

"This guy is relentless!" Adrenaline coursed through her.

"It's not safe to stay here," Zach said.

Gracie nodded. "On a good note, he doesn't appear interested in the horses at all."

"Great, a killer with a conscience," Cameron grunted.

"I'm sorry, but Zach's right. The cabins aren't safe for us to stay in."

"Let's load up supplies, then move to the bunker," Cameron replied.

"I'll keep watch while you two grab what you need." Zach hurried out, Amber at his side.

Gracie and Cameron headed for his cabin, but he took a sharp right and strode toward the property gate.

"What's wrong?" Gracie asked.

Cameron didn't reply—instead, he approached the barrier in cautious movements. Gracie hurried to catch up with him and spotted the manila envelope perched against the iron bars.

"Don't touch it. Let me look first," she said, pushing ahead of him.

She kneeled and withdrew the envelope, carefully using her sleeve to cover her hand. When she had pulled it free, Gracie placed it on the ground, then repositioned it to unlock the clasp and open it without getting her fingerprints on it. She tilted the envelope, sliding out the content. A homemade card with a sad face on the front that read, *I see you've found someone new. I hope she's worth it.*

Cameron's face blanched and he shook his head. "Delilah."

"Has she done this before?" Gracie asked.

"Yeah, but she never signs anything. I can't prove it's her."

"Based on what I found about her prior incidents, she's learning to keep her activities more surreptitious to avoid charges," Gracie admitted. She put thc items together and lifted them, ensuring her fingers didn't directly touch the paper. "It's not a threat, but in light of all that's happened, and the last sentence, I think it's worth having it fingerprinted."

"It won't show anything. She's careful," Cameron said, defeat in his tone.

"How do you know that?"

Cameron shrugged.

"Guess she took the relationship more seriously than you did?"

"Apparently." Cameron snorted.

"The timing is suspicious. Do you think Delilah is behind the shooting? Would she hire someone to do it for her?" Gracie asked, tossing out the idea.

"I'm not sure dumping her qualifies me for death. However, she wasn't always a rational person."

"Jealousy and revenge are powerful motives," Gracie said.

"Don't I know it? It's how I got here in the first place. Just wish Bane had caught up with the shooter so this would be over."

"He probably would've caught him, but I couldn't let Bane go after an armed person like that," Gracie explained. "The risk was too high that the guy might've shot him."

"I understand."

"Honestly, the shooter's smart and probably counted on that factor."

"He knows I'll return here for the horses, too," Cameron acknowledged.

Gracie hadn't considered that. "It's feasible."

"Relationships complicate every situation. If Delilah is behind this, like you're saying, it makes me realize it's better to be alone, right?" Cameron faced her. "I mean, she thinks you're my new girlfriend. Isn't that ridiculous?"

"Yeah." Gracie shoved down the hurt from his comment. "Romance isn't my thing," she mumbled.

"Mine either. Can you imagine how dangerous this would be if I had someone special in my life? If Delilah is on some revenge mission, she's targeting both of us. If you weren't an armed deputy marshal, we might be dead already. No way." He shook his head. "Whew. So glad that's not the case. In a moment, I could lose everything all over again."

His overemphasis in averting love niggled at Gracie. What did that mean? "Yeah," Gracie said again halfheartedly. Except she didn't agree.

Her heart was shifting without her approval. When she'd talked with Zach earlier, she realized she'd missed out on a future with someone she loved. She thought back to the silly song they'd shared and the fun in the cabin only moments before.

Now, for whatever illogical reason, Gracie desperately wanted to know the joy of commitment, and experience marriage, children, and a family of her own. In that moment, she allowed herself the freedom to admit that's what she wanted all along. Her parents had provided a great example for she and Leigh.

"Ready?" Cameron asked, holding a duffel bag.

Gracie turned, staring at him. She froze... How had it happened? Gracie was ready to take a chance at the worst possible time for a man who had no interest in her.

Cameron wasn't in emotional agreement with her.

But Gracie was changing. She wanted the happily-ever-after that included being loved.

Except she'd done it again.

Gracie Fitzgerald was falling for the wrong guy. And she couldn't afford another broken heart.

* * *

Cameron led Gracie and Zach to the underground bunker he'd built at the edge of his property. The project had taken him several months to complete, which he'd done in stages to maintain its secrecy. The entrance appeared as a root cellar, encased in a hill, blending with the scenery. The second hidden door at the rear permitted a clandestine exit. Cameron shot a glance at the dogs. "There is a ladder we have to climb down."

"Not a problem," Gracie replied. "We can military carry them. Bane." The Malinois moved to her side immediately, and she hoisted him over her shoulders, allowing his paws to hang on either side of her head.

Zach did the same with Amber.

Cameron opened the door and began the descent. Zach and Gracie trailed behind him. When they reached the bottom, they set down the dogs and Cameron climbed up, securing the doors from the inside.

The half-cylindrical room, with its rounded top and sides, was constructed of metal with a concrete foundation.

"Wow," Zach said. "This is nice."

"No kidding." Gracie removed her backpack, placing it near the entrance.

The single room housed a sofa, bunkbeds for two and a small kitchenette.

"Thanks. I found the plans online and the rest came together easily."

Zach and Gracie settled onto the sofa and the dogs lounged on the large carpet. Cameron dragged over a chair from the two-person dining table and sat down. "There's a rear emergency exit." He gestured toward the small alcove to the farthest side. "It's nothing more than a hole in the ground with a ladder, but it's well concealed on the outside."

"We'll hunker down for the night here," Zach said. "Tomorrow, we need to make more effort to hunt down this shooter before he finds us again."

Cameron sighed. "What could I have possibly done to deserve that much hatred?"

Gracie updated Zach on the envelope they'd found. "She could've hired someone to go after Cameron," she proposed.

"It's not unheard of. A woman scorned and all that," Zach agreed. "Any idea who the shooter is in relation to Delilah?"

"A hired thug?" Cameron asked.

"I'm thinking she went to someone closer to her." Gracie met his eyes.

"Like?" Cameron made no effort to hide his skepticism.

"Delilah's persuasive, right?" Gracie asked.

"She's got an upbeat personality, at first," Cameron said.

"Then we can't discount the possibility," Gracie advised. "And if she met up with someone who has ill feelings toward you, they'd bond over the common enemy factor."

"Anyone fit that bill?" Zach asked.

Cameron shook his head.

"Yes," Gracie replied at the same time.

"Who?" Cameron pinned her with a stare.

"Arlee Gross. He's a disgruntled employee who lost custody and visitation privileges to see his child," Gracie said. "That's a pretty big motivator."

"Agreed," Zach said.

"You've got it all wrong. The guy was upset, but he's not a murderer," Cameron countered, though doubts warred with his heart. Did anyone believe a person they knew would murder another human? Until Quigley had proven that theory, Cameron never would've suspected the man was capable.

"Whoever the shooter is, they're determined," Zach said.

"The attacks appear rage motivated," Gracie said. "He's using heavy firepower, and considering there were two law-enforcement officers in that cabin, he's got moxie. The guy shot up the entire building, not caring who he hit."

Zach added, "That speaks to emotion behind the act."

"Or desperation to finish the job so he painted with a wide brush," Cameron snapped. A headache throbbed at the front of his skull, and he got to his feet. "It's late and it's been a long day."

"Yeah, a little sleep is in order," Zach replied with a yawn.

Gracie yawned, too. "The power of suggestion is amazing."

"You two take the bunk beds, I'll sleep on the

sofa," Cameron said, grateful to end the discussion for a while.

They shifted positions, Gracie taking the top bunk and Zach the lower. Cameron stretched out on the sofa and dimmed the lights.

In the dark, his mind raced, and disbelief hung in his thoughts. Arlee wasn't that kind of man. Was he? What about the envelope Delilah had left? Why hire someone and then announce herself? He rolled over, shoving away the images, hurt, regrets and everything in between.

At last, sleep embraced Cameron.

A guttural growl had him bolting upright. How long had he slept?

In the ambient glow of the nightlights, he spotted Bane and Amber on all fours, facing the rear alcove. Gracie slowly lowered herself from the top bunk, Zach joining her. They withdrew their guns, holding them in the ready position.

The trio remained quiet except for the dogs.

Gracie and Zach offered hand signals and both animals silenced, but no one moved.

All at once, the back door flew open and smoke filled the bunker.

"Bane, *fass*!" Gracie ordered.

Cameron didn't recognize the unfamiliar word, but the dog lunged toward the door, blasting through the smoke unhindered.

The form of a man wearing a ski mask appeared in the mist. The fog kept them from seeing clearly.

Somehow, he must've messed with the electricity, preventing them from turning on any lights.

A scream from the intruder, then a gunshot blast.

"Bane! Come!" Gracie called.

The dog returned to her side.

Several rounds erupted in the dark.

A burning sensation pierced Cameron's shoulder and he cried out. "I'm hit."

Gracie moved to his side. "Zach, stay with Cameron. We're going after this guy!"

Zach took her place. "Let me see where you're shot."

They stepped back, allowing Gracie to hoist Bane onto her shoulders.

"Later! Go through the front, he'll expect you to come out the back," Cameron grunted.

"I'll cover you on the rear exit. Stay here," Zach said. He climbed the ladder as Gracie and Bane sprinted for the front entrance and climbed the ladder.

Cameron sat dazed for several seconds. The smoke was finally clearing, but the smell of gunpowder filled his senses, burning his nose. He compressed the wound with his hand and searched for the battery-operated lantern. Gunshots outside told him Zach and Gracie were battling the intruder.

He found the light source just as Zach slid down the ladder. "How're you doing?"

"Go with Gracie!" Cameron barked. "She needs backup!"

"She's got this," Zach replied too calmly for Cameron's taste.

"The guy's relentless."

"Gracie's a great cop and Bane's a fantastic K-9." Zach moved closer. "They'll be fine," he insisted. "I need to check your wound."

"I've been better," Cameron grunted, carrying the lamp to the table and allowing Zach to inspect the injury.

"Looks like a nasty graze," Zach said.

"Good. The last thing I want is surgery to remove a bullet." Cameron stared at the wall past Zach. "And don't even think about calling an ambulance or taking me to the hospital."

"It's not bad enough to warrant that," Zach assured.

"We need to go help Gracie."

"We're not any help to her if you're hurt," Zach argued, his tone steely. "Too-many-cooks-in-the-kitchen kind of thing."

Cameron harrumphed. What he couldn't tell Zach was that he'd messed up, by pushing Gracie away at every turn. "If something happens to her..."

"It won't." Zach attempted to ease Cameron's stress but until Gracie returned, he wouldn't rest. No matter what he told himself about emotionally distancing from Gracie, his heart refused to listen and the fear of losing her was too great to bear.

NINE

Darkness pressed in all around Gracie, enclosing her in shadows and broken only by the glow of her flashlight beam bouncing ahead of her and Bane. They bolted through the woods, pushing through low-hanging branches, and stumbling over fallen logs and the uneven ground in search of the intruder. Bane's forward momentum indicated he'd found the scent and she'd not disturb him. "Don't lose it, buddy. We gotta catch this guy."

Gunshots blasted at her, and they dove for cover.

Something pricked her calf.

Gracie returned fire, holding Bane close. They waited for several seconds then continued the pursuit.

Bane's nose never left the ground as he sniffed his way, zigzagging through the woods. But as the dog slowed, Gracie understood they were losing the shooter. Concern for Cameron jabbed her heart with intensity and fear. She shoved away the thoughts, forcing herself to focus on the mission right in front of her. Until they caught the shooter, Cameron would never be safe.

Zach was with him, and he'd make sure Cameron got the care he needed.

"Come on, Bane. *Zook*," she ordered. The Malinois paused, sniffing the air, moving to the right, then the left. They reached a creek and she feared he'd stop, but the dog continued forward, and she sprinted after him.

The intruder was fast, or he'd taken another route. Either way, he'd left his scent on this trail. If he'd driven in on an ATV, he'd escape before they caught up. She shoved away the thoughts. No. She and Bane were professional trackers. They'd catch him.

Her legs ached from exertion, but she kept up with Bane. When he increased his pace, Gracie pushed on, ignoring the pain. They ran hard and fast, exiting the woods beyond Pronghorn Hills and entering Badlands National Park again. The elegant stone formations rose around her, enveloping Gracie.

Frustration filled her again as Bane slowed, sniffing the air, then the ground, shifting uncertainly from side to side. All signs he was losing the scent. But he'd found it before, and he'd do it again.

Help us, Lord. The prayer flowed in her mind as easily as breathing.

After they'd walked a little farther without signs of the intruder, Gracie called off the search. Bane would continue as long as she allowed, but his indecisiveness proved the effort was futile.

"Bane." The dog reluctantly returned to her side.

"You did good, buddy. It's okay." Exhausted, she turned, allowing her flashlight to illuminate the area. The barren landscape offered few places of protection, leaving them exposed. If the shooter had night-vision goggles, he'd easily spot them.

She scarcely breathed. Only the chirrups of crickets and an owl hooting in the distance reached her ears.

A shuffle in the distance had the tiny hairs on the back of her neck rising in visceral response. Gracie shut off her flashlight and pulled Bane closer to her behind a boulder. The sensation that they weren't alone had Gracie hesitating. Without shelter to conceal them, they were left unshielded. Determining it was unsafe, Gracie and Bane retraced their steps in the dark, starting toward the ranch.

Another soft snap had her pausing to look. Bane emitted a low growl and stared out into the distance, adding to her fear. Gracie twisted and stepped wrong. The crunching sound from her ankle preceded her muffled cry. She dropped to the ground, clutching her left ankle. *Please don't let it be broken.* Bane moved to her side, nudging her arm. "I'm okay," she whispered reassuringly to him. After several long seconds, the pain slowly morphed into a solid throbbing, bearable but uncomfortable. Gracie slowly pulled herself to her feet, testing her weight on the injured ankle. She winced and began walking with her teeth clenched to keep from emitting any sounds.

The trek to Pronghorn Hills was slow and painful. Gracie stopped several times to gather the energy and fortitude to keep going. She couldn't call for help, so her only choice was trudging through the woods.

When they'd created enough distance, Gracie turned on the flashlight, allowing them to see the rugged terraine clearer. By the time she neared the edge of Cameron's property a good hour later, Gracie's adrenaline waned, and tension tightened her neck and shoulders. Her ankle still ached, but she'd not let it stop her.

At last, she spotted the rear exit of the bunker and hobbled forward. "Come on, Bane."

Defeat hung in her dog's demeanor. He was made for the chase and the win. He'd lost the intruder, and it showed in his slumped head.

"We'll get him." She stroked his velvety ears. Gracie lifted the door, and dim light leaked out. "It's just me," she called down. "But I need help with Bane."

Silcnce.

Fear consumed Gracie. Where had they gone?

"Here!" Zach hurried to her side with Cameron who pulled her into his arms in a tight embrace. Stunned, she glanced over his shoulder at Zach, who stood stupefied, as well.

When Cameron finally released his hold, he stepped back. "Sorry. I just… Are you okay?"

Gracie blinked, still unsure how to process that reaction. "Sort of, I hurt my ankle."

"We moved to the cabin," Zach explained.

"Lean on me, I'll help you." Cameron stepped beside her, allowing Gracie to put her weight on him. "Did you catch him?"

The words she dreaded addressing. Gracie shook her head. "No. He made a quick escape, which proves he's familiar with the area. I'm thinking a hidden ATV or something because Bane lost his scent. He obviously knows how to throw us off his trail."

"What happened to your ankle?" Cameron asked. The freshness of his soap mingled with a musk scent, and she fought the urge not to inhale deeper.

"I stepped wrong and twisted my ankle. It's okay."

They reached Cameron's cabin, and he helped her to the sofa. Gracie slumped onto the cushion, relieved to be off her leg. "Let me look at it."

Zach hurried into the kitchen and returned with an ice pack.

"It's fine." She waved off Cameron and slowly untied her boot, removing it. She gingerly touched the ankle. "A little swollen but not broken."

"You have X-ray vision?" Cameron asked sarcastically.

Gracie noticed the bandage on Cameron's bare shoulder for the first time. Crimson stained the fabric of the light-colored T-shirt. She blinked.

"Nothing but a graze," he said, picking up on her body language.

"The perp cut the electricity, but we found the spot and put a temporary repair on the wires," Zach said.

"Are you sure the bullet didn't penetrate your shoulder?" Gracie asked Cameron.

"No, it stings but I'll survive," he replied nonchalantly.

"We should take you to the hospital," she insisted.

"I think that would be better served for your injury," he replied.

"I'm fine," she grunted.

"Yep, so am I," he argued.

They held a silent standoff, staring one another down.

"Wow, it's like two ends of the same stubborn human," Zach teased. "You both need medical examination."

"Negative," Gracie replied.

"I'll call the team to notify them while you two argue about not going to the hospital," Zach said.

Gracie laughed. "Okay, then." A dull ache above her ankle had her shifting slightly. Her fingers skimmed the pant-leg fabric and came back wet. "I must've cut it on something. It doesn't really hurt, though."

Cameron kneeled, rolling up her pant leg. "Gracie, you're bleeding." Concern tinged his tone, and worry filled his eyes.

Like an instant reaction to the word and the dampness on her skin, a burning sensation erupted from the back of her calf. She leaned over, doing her best to inspect the injury.

"Let me see." Zach moved beside them, using a

flashlight to examine the wound. "It's a through-and-through bullet wound."

"Why is it just now hurting?" Gracie gripped her leg.

"Adrenaline dump," Zach said.

"Let's get to the bathroom. I've got supplies." Cameron jumped up, helping Gracie to stand and lean on him as they headed down the hallway.

Though she could hobble along fine, she relished his touch and the personal care.

"You need a bandage change," she said.

They entered the bathroom and Cameron helped her to sit on the edge of the tub. He kneeled and began cleansing the wound with antiseptic. She winced, gritting her teeth against the sting. Worse, Gracie tried not to react to Cameron's touch as he gently bandaged her leg. His strong hand touched her calf muscle, and she was grateful to be sitting. Her body felt like gelatin, and she wanted to melt, but she kept herself in check.

He's a witness. You're a cop. Leave it alone.

"Okay, thanks," she said a little too quickly. "My turn."

They traded places, and Gracie assumed nurse duties for him. She carefully dabbed a cotton ball on the disinfectant, then cleansed his shoulder wound.

He winced. "You're doing that to get me back."

"Me?" She feigned innocence. "Never."

"Yeah, right," he grunted good-naturedly.

Gracie applied an antibiotic ointment with a

pain-killing agent and replaced the gauze and tape. "The bullet sure left a nasty mark, but thankfully, it didn't penetrate the skin."

"Feels like a massive burn."

"Mine, too." Her hands pressed carefully on the tape, securing it to Cameron's skin. Strength oozed from his pores and his muscles were taut beneath her fingertips.

The significance of all that had occurred hit her like a boulder between the eyes. Cameron could've died. The intruder's aim was good.

Too good.

What if Cameron's injury had been more than a grazing? What if he'd been killed?

Gracie's chest tightened, the what-if scenarios squeezing her like a vise.

She couldn't lose him.

He turned to face her. "Hey, are you all right?"

She paused, meeting his gaze.

They held their positions.

Gracie's pulse quickened, and she tried to avert her eyes, but Cameron's irises consumed her, drinking her in.

Neither spoke.

Finally, Cameron cleared his throat and looked down. "Thanks."

"Right." Gracie swallowed hard and blurted, "That's a bummer. These were my favorite cargo pants." She gestured toward her leg.

"They look good on you." As though realizing what he'd said, Cameron cleared his throat. "Anyway, don't the marshals provide some kind of clothing allowance?"

"Yeah. Perks of the job." She smiled.

"You're great at it." His intense gaze held hers.

Gracie looked away. "I found solace in my career after my family died… I couldn't help myself, but I could help others."

"You remained broken, though," Cameron said.

"Yeah, I suppose so. My ex betrayed me bigtime."

"You mentioned that earlier, but I didn't want to be nosy."

Gracie picked at her cuticles to avoid meeting his eyes. She thought about how Cameron had spent more than a decade alone and recognized she needed to tell him the rest of her story. In fact, she wanted to share it with him. Inhaling a fortifying breath, she said, "Rod and I met while I was working a case. He's a first responder, too, so it was a common connection for us. We got serious fast and moved in together." She hesitated, working up the courage to finish the story. Nothing like confessing her most embarrassing moments aloud. "I'd never done that before, and it was against my beliefs, but I looked at pleasing him more than staying true to myself. That was a huge mistake."

She shook her head. "Anyway, I assumed he'd propose as the next logical step. He didn't. Instead, I caught him making out with a female deputy and learned he'd been seeing her on the side nearly the entire time we were together. I felt used and foolish."

Cameron shook his head. "I'm so sorry and I don't know Rod, but he's an idiot. He had the most beautiful woman in the world, and he blew it."

Gracie's head shot upright so fast she felt the zing down her spine. Their gazes held for several long seconds and her pulse thrummed. "You're sweet to say that."

"Just speaking the truth." He didn't avert his eyes and Gracie's pulse quickened yet again.

Then Cameron asked lightly, "What happened? Did you burn all his stuff on the front lawn?"

She smiled despite the seriousness of the conversation. "No. But the thought crossed my mind." She chuckled. "Anyway, it was a good wake-up call for me. I'd compromised my principles for a man, and I vowed never to do that again. The whole thing helped me reestablish my boundaries. But the pain remained so after Rod shattered my heart, I dove into my job full-throttle. I took extended cases that kept me working massive amounts of overtime. My job is a safe place for me to invest myself because it's the one familiar thing I have." She bit her lip as the emotion rose. Kenyon's death and meeting Cam had opened her eyes and awakened something inside her she'd tried hard to repress. Gracie fixed her gaze on him. "I want more than a career at the end of the day. Kenyon, a fellow officer who died, had children, and as awful as it is they were orphaned, I believe he loved them to the fullest. My parents were amazing, and I cherish every second I had with them."

Cameron cleared his throat. "But you were wrong about Rod. Doesn't that scare you?"

"Rod made his betraying choices, I didn't. I was honest with him." If she stopped and chickened out from confessing her thoughts, she'd never have a second chance when they relocated him. Even if he said no, she had to try. "One thing I realized when it happened was, I was more humiliated by my behavior and how my colleagues would view me. They'd think I was a bad judge of character."

"Did they react the way you'd imagined?"

"Not at all. I also realized that God alone is where my trust and affirmation need to come from. I was looking at everyone but Him."

He studied her, appearing to take in her words.

Zach's voice carried to them, interrupting the moment, and Gracie overheard him updating the team with information that the intruder had escaped capture again. She cringed. She and Bane were two for two on failing to capture the intruder. This creep was ruining her perfect record. That had to change. And it started with her getting her head on straight and remembering her priorities.

But with Cameron sitting beside her, Gracie could barely focus. This couldn't happen again. She'd already walked this path, and her bad judgment had shattered her heart. But Cameron wasn't Rod.

Yet, the situation reeked of similarity.

Had the shooter escaped because Gracie's mind bounced around ridiculous romantic notions when she should've concentrated on tracking the criminal? She had no one to blame but herself.

And it had to stop now.

"Ready?" Cameron asked, regaining her attention.

Gracie nodded, quickly rolling down her pant leg. "Thanks."

He helped her to her room, and she dropped onto the mattress.

"Gracie?"

"Yeah?"

"True confessions, right?"

"Okay." Her pulse increased again.

"You scared me."

"I did?" She tilted her head, confused.

"You were gone so long. I thought something bad happened to you." Cameron swallowed hard.

Gracie's heart squeezed. "You were worried about me?"

"More than that. Terrified you'd..." He didn't finish the sentence. He didn't need to.

Zach returned, eliminating the option to continue the discussion. "Team's got the latest. Amber and I will take first shift, keeping watch. You two need to rest."

"I'll set an alarm to trade shifts with you," Gracie blurted, face warming. Had he overheard them talking?

"No rush." Zach and Amber disappeared, his footsteps moving away.

Bane hopped onto the bed beside her.

"Well, good night." Cameron turned on his heel and exited the room, closing the door behind him.

Gracie scooted back, leaning against the headboard. Her mind whirled out of control.

She thanked God in a silent prayer that though they'd sustained wounds, they were superficial, albeit painful.

Her thoughts returned to Cameron. *Lord, help me.*

His intrusion into her heart terrified Gracie. He wasn't just a witness. She cared about him, and in that moment, Gracie vowed to do whatever it took to protect him and find the shooter.

Even if it meant pretending she wasn't falling hard for him.

Cameron rolled to his side, gazing out the window. Morning sunlight poured into his room, filling it with warmth and the promise of a new day. Yet, on its heels, dread that the unrelenting danger still lurked left him discouraged. He'd lain awake for a while, but dragging himself out of bed lacked appeal.

He groaned, remembering what he'd confessed to Gracie the night before. What was he thinking? Cameron had no right to tell her how he felt, and the idea of facing her this morning brought on foreboding.

The sound of voices carried to him. Gracie and Zach were up and moving. His three-bedroom cabin allowed sleeping space for his guests, though he wondered how much either had rested in the night. Strangely, he'd never used the spare rooms before, and he was grateful to have thought ahead enough to prepare for such an occasion.

It was still early, but Cameron never slept this late. Feeling like a slacker, he forced himself out of bed and hurried to get ready for the day.

By the time he entered the kitchen, Gracie and Zach were cooking. His stomach growled as he inhaled the aroma of pancakes and bacon.

"I'm not used to this." Cameron poured himself a cup of coffee.

"The dogs have internal clocks, so we were up early," Gracie replied.

He leaned against the counter. "Sorry for sleeping in."

"Don't be," Zach said. "Besides, when's the last time you got to rest?"

The pointed question hit Cameron hard. "Not since I first suspected someone was after me."

"How long was that?" Gracie asked.

"A few weeks."

"That's what we figured," she replied. The tenderness in her eyes nearly undid Cameron.

Zach stacked a plate high with pancakes. "Breakfast is ready."

The trio moved to the table and settled into their chairs while the dogs lounged on the rug, sprawled on their sides with legs outstretched. Both panted softly.

"They got an early morning run," Gracie explained. "They're content."

"You ran?" Cameron asked, forking a bite.

"Yeah, we did a perimeter check combined with morning exercise," Gracie replied. "It worked well."

All while he slept and hid out in his room because he didn't want to face her. *Way to go, Cameron.*

Gracie's cell phone rang and she withdrew it, glancing at the screen. "It's Cheyenne."

Cameron recognized the name and scoured his brain. Oh, yes, she was their technical specialist or something like that.

"Hey, Cheyenne, I'm putting you on speakerphone." Gracie activated the feature and placed the device on the center of the table. "Please repeat what you just said."

"Sure, hi Zach and Cameron," a bodiless voice said. "I ran Barry Noonan's information and discovered he's out of town. He did a live TV event in New York super early this morning, so there's no way he could've been at your location last night."

"Well, that narrows down our list," Gracie replied. "Anything else?"

"Not really. I'll keep digging."

"Thanks," Gracie said, and disconnected.

"Delilah's still as a possible suspect if she hired someone, like Arlee Gross or Phillip Quigley," Zach chimed in, biting into a piece of bacon.

"Or they acted apart from her," Gracie added.

Cameron remained silent, not trusting himself

to contribute to the discussion. His cell phone rang and he rushed to his bedroom to answer it.

A text from Delilah. Coffee?

He groaned—the woman could not take a hint.

"Cam?" Gracie called. "Everything okay?"

He walked out to the dining room and showed her the phone. "Normally, I'd ignore it, but do you think I should reply? If you believe she's behind these attacks, do we need to get information from her?"

Gracie and Zach exchanged glances.

Hello? A second message from Delilah.

"Is it normal for her to keep persisting if you delay responding?" Gracie asked.

"Yeah."

"Let it build," Zach said.

I can see you're too busy with your new girlfriend to respond. Delilah texted.

"Go ahead and answer," Gracie suggested.

"What do I say?" Cameron held out the phone.

Gracie took it, then typed a response. What makes you think that? Are you stalking me?

No response.

"She's watching the house," Zach said.

"Yep." Gracie handed Cameron the phone. "If she responds, which she won't, let me know."

Cameron pocketed the device, glancing disinterestedly at his breakfast. "I lost my appetite."

"Eat up, anyway. It'll keep you going," Zach suggested.

The trio finished the meal and cleaned up in record time.

"Let's do a little digging of our own." Gracie brought her laptop to the table and Cameron watched as she scrolled through the internet, finding multiple sources on Delilah, Arlee and Phillip.

"Delilah is a busy lady," Zach said. "She's got pictures of her with several guys in various locations. Recently, too."

They scrolled through Delilah's active social media feed where she had posed provocatively with different men.

"Looks like she's trying too hard to prove they like her," Gracie replied. "It's almost as if she's posting them to get someone's attention." She looked at Cameron. "Like yours."

"As in make me jealous?"

"Yes."

"Hmm, although that doesn't prove anything," Gracie added. "She could be pining for Cameron while she's dating half the town."

"True." Zach grunted.

Gracie's cell rang again, and she put the call on speakerphone. "Hey, Cheyenne."

"I checked into Arlee Gross," Cheyenne replied. "The guy closed his bank account and his credit cards have been inactive since his employment termination date. So he's got no electronic paper or financial trail."

"Yeah and his social media is pictures of him with his kids," Gracie said.

"What about Delilah?" Zach asked.

"She's an enigma," Cheyenne replied. "Active on social media, has several different checking accounts, but she doesn't have a lot of money."

"Why spread out her funds? Wouldn't leaving them in one account to build interest be a smarter move?" Gracie asked.

"You'd think so, but she has no major purchases, and she maintains a low balance after her paycheck is direct-deposited. Looks like she works for a big-box store near there," Cheyenne said. When she read off the name, Gracie and Zach exchanged a look.

"That's the same store Hobart works at," Gracie said.

"Could be coincidental. It's the largest employer between here and Black Hawk," Zach replied.

"Hmm. Maybe."

Cameron watched the interaction, picking up on the importance of each lead. The investigative side fascinated him.

"She immediately withdraws the same amount of money every month and has for a couple of years," Cheyenne reported.

"She might pay cash for everything," Zach countered.

"Thanks, Cheyenne," Gracie replied, disconnecting.

Cameron sat back in the chair. "Now what?"

"I'm liking Delilah for this, but it doesn't explain how or why she discovered your real identity," Gracie said.

"And she didn't mention that in her recent text," Cameron replied.

"She wouldn't because that would reveal she was behind the attacks, but it gives her leverage," Gracie said. "Sounds like she's still trying to keep on your good side."

"Now, let's see if we can find out about Phillip's life." Gracie pulled up several social media apps, searching for Phillip.

Cameron and Zach did the same, using other social media avenues.

"Hmm, Phillip's relationship status reads single," Gracie said.

"I saw that, I'm searching through his photos and found several with a woman, just need her name," Zach said, scrolling on his phone.

"Found her," Cameron announced. "Stephanie Cramer."

The trio worked together scouring the internet.

"Don't you love people who are willing to use the World Wide Web as their personal diary?" Zach snorted.

"Yeah, Stephanie is telling all," Gracie replied. "She's used every word for *liar* on the planet."

"Listen to this," Cameron said. "'Don't believe your man until you've verified everything.' Wonder what that's all about?"

"I think I've found it," Gracie said. "She wrote this last week. 'I believed every word he said but when @PhilyQ promised a ring he never delivered, I learned why. He's broke. He should've spent more money on acting lessons instead. Then maybe I wouldn't have seen through his rich-boy facade.' Ouch."

"Right?" Zach chuckled. "Let's check out @PhilyQ's financials."

Cameron marveled at how easy it was for them to trace Phillip Quigley's locations, comings and goings, basically every time the man sneezed via social media. "This is why I stay away from the internet," he said as they compiled their findings.

"Well, that and living in WITSEC," Gracie teased.

"It was a huge motivator," he replied with a grin.

Cameron loved her attitude, her sense of humor. And all of it was packaged in a beautiful woman. *Knock it off.*

"Whoa, get this," Gracie said, regaining his attention. "Phillip filed for bankruptcy because he lost out on a big project. Looks like his real estate company owes millions."

"I'd call that motive," Zach replied.

"Yep."

"But Phillip has had twelve years to search for me," Cameron argued. "That still doesn't answer how he found me or why."

"He lost his lucrative California-based luxury vacation home business, his girlfriend and most likely his lifestyle," Gracie said.

"He's using me as a scapegoat for his troubles," Cameron mused.

"Perhaps he blames you for starting his life's failures," Zach said. "After his father went to prison for murder, his family name was smeared, his lifestyle changed and now he's bankrupt and single."

"And with Stephanie smearing his name again, he's not bachelor of the year," Gracie said.

"We can't stick around. Regardless if it's Phillip or someone else, the person is becoming more determined," Zach said. "We need to leave the ranch."

"I'll contact my boss and request a safehouse location," Gracie replied.

As each moved to make their calls, Cameron's heart sank. His dad had once told him your enemies aren't people you hate, it's the people who hate you. Whatever Phillip, or if not him, the real assassin, thought, Cameron was his enemy. And he planned to eliminate Cameron and anyone else who got in his way. He couldn't risk Gracie's life anymore. Even if it meant losing everything he cared about.

She meant more.

"Well, good news and bad news," Gracie said. "We have a safehouse location, but we can't get in until tomorrow. We'll have to stay here one more night."

"What if the assailant returns?" Cameron asked.

The trio shared a glance. They'd survived too many attempts on their lives. They might not survive another. It would be the longest twenty-four hours ever waiting for a killer hunting them.

TEN

"Cameron!"

He jolted upright in the bed at Gracie's urgent cry and threw off the covers, sprinting from his bedroom.

"The horses are gone!" Gracie stood at his door.

His biggest fears realized, Cameron rushed back to his room and shoved his bare feet into his boots. Thankful he'd worn his jeans to bed, he snagged the closest shirt and hurried to join Gracie. Why hadn't he asked Joel to get the horses last night? Because he was selfish, wanting as much time with them as possible before handing them over to his friend.

"Please let them be okay..." The prayer escaped his lips before his mind registered, he'd spoken.

"Zane went to search for them by vehicle." Gracie leashed Bane and they sprinted from the cabin.

"Have you checked the stables?"

"Yes, Zach was out early with the dogs and noticed the pen door standing wide open."

"Why didn't I have Joel pick them up last night?"

Cameron groaned, spotting the broken pen door. It faced the opposite side of the stable, keeping it from the cabin's visual range. He pushed aside the remnants of the door and stepped inside. *Don't panic. Think.*

"Do you have any idea where they'd run to?" Gracie's phone rang. "It's Zach."

He turned, anxious, as she activated the speakerphone. "I found them. They're wandering north of Badlands National Park," Zach said.

"We're on our way." Cameron spun on his heel and hurried to the stable, where he gathered the lead ropes.

He and Gracie raced through the property and out to the park. Neither spoke as they ran the lengthy distance, finally entering the Badlands and locating Zach's vehicle on a road to the east.

Rocket and Sugar grazed lazily amid the desert-like grounds.

"Stay calm, they feed off your energy," Cameron explained. "Leave the dogs here, they might spook the animals and send them running."

Gracie and Zach ordered the dogs to sit and stay. Cameron hoped that would be enough to keep them stationary.

He handed a rope to Gracie and gestured for her to go the opposite of him, so they could circle the horses.

"What're you two doing?" Cameron said, forcing quietness into his tone. "Out wandering?"

Rocket looked up at his approach and snorted, taking two steps back.

"Aw, c'mon, buddy. I need to get you home safe," Cameron said as he approached slowly. He gently inched toward the horse and managed to get the lead rope around the animal. "Good boy, Rocket," he cooed. "Gracie, come take this rope while I work with Sugar."

"Okay." Her voice was light, and she closed the distance between them cautiously.

Once she had the lead rope, Cameron moved toward Sugar. She eyed him suspiciously. "Hey, girl, you're all right." Again, keeping a quiet voice, he maneuvered the lead rope, securing her.

"I'll take the dogs back and meet you at the ranch. We'll do recon before you return," Zach advised.

"Thanks," Gracie said, leading Rocket.

Exhaling relief, she and Cameron started toward the ranch.

"What purpose did that serve?" Cameron asked, maintaining a calm demeanor though anger boiled within him. "Why release them into the wild?"

"Playing games with us," Gracie surmised.

"A warning to let me know he's watching."

"Or she."

"You think Delilah's responsible?"

"Possibly." Gracie shrugged. "At least the animals aren't hurt. The move was intended to upset you."

"Kudos to them." Bitterness lingered in Cameron's words. "It worked."

The steady clomping of the horses' hooves on the ground soothed Cameron. He reached up, offering a petting of Sugar's muzzle. "Good girl."

"We got through a quiet night, it figures this would happen," Gracie said.

"No kidding." Cameron shook his head.

They didn't speak the rest of the walk, and Cameron was grateful. By the time they'd secured the horses in the stable and repaired the pen, the sun had fully risen in the sky.

"I need to put a few things together. I'll meet you guys in the cabin," Cameron said, politely excusing himself.

"Sure." Gracie offered an understanding nod, ushering Zach and the dogs toward the cabin.

Reassured he was alone, Cameron strolled the stables and leaned against the far wall. He bowed his head. "Lord, I'm not sure how I feel about You. But I'm desperate." Wasn't that what drove most people to their knees?

No audible voice offered comfort and Cameron shoved off the wall. He stepped outside, rounding the stables and gazed out at the Pronghorn Hills Guest Ranch. He'd had such big plans for this place. The business had taken off faster than he'd anticipated, and he'd kept busy with plenty of guests and daily duties that he'd not had time to do the desired renovations on the cabins. The sense of leaving the place unfinished irked him like a mosquito bite.

If only he could at least complete the restorations he'd begun, he wouldn't have as many issues leaving.

Liar. No matter when he left, it would hit him hard.

Reminded of the reasons he'd be forced to vacate, Cameron surveyed the forested land at the edge of the property in search of danger. He'd never shaken the feeling that someone was watching him. Paranoia or a good self-awareness? He wasn't sure, but it never fully disappeared.

A chill carried on the early morning breeze and birds chirped happily from their hiding places amid the trees. Though he longed to stay and enjoy the quiet, he'd opt to maximize every moment he had. He returned to the stable, inhaling the sweet scent of hay, combined with the earthy aroma of the animals.

"I'm going to miss you, Rocket." He leaned against the stall where Rocket stood peering, head hovering over the door. Cameron gently approached, offering a scratch to the animal's velvety muzzle.

Sugar offered a whinny and Cameron chuckled. "Don't worry, I wouldn't leave you out," he cooed, giving her the same affection.

Like a vise around his chest, Cameron grappled with the pain and worry over his ranch and animals. "You two probably worked up an appetite with your big adventure this morning."

Was it possible Gracie could arrest the attacker

and the Marshals would permit Cameron to stay remain status quo? The hope hurt more than the sorrow of leaving, yet Cameron clung to the single thread.

He offered each horse one last pat, then walked to the tack room, and tugged the door open. The familiarity of the stables brought comfort and the routine helped him to focus on the present. This place had been his favorite reprieve anytime he was on the ranch. In the presence of the animals, Cameron was free to be authentic, without fear of repercussions or judgment. Riding alone, he'd bared his soul to them individually. They'd provided the emotional support that only comes from the genuine heart of an animal.

Cameron tugged on his leather work gloves, then scooped out the required specialized grain formula he used for Rocket and carried it to his stall. He set down the container and swung open the door. The horse took a half step to the side, allowing Cameron to enter. "Buddy, I suppose deep down we both knew the day might come when we'd have to part. I just wanted to pretend it wouldn't happen." His throat constricted with sadness and Cameron focused on pouring the feed and then exited the space.

The hay rustled beneath the horse's powerful hooves as he shifted to enjoy his breakfast.

Cameron returned to the tack room and repeated the process for Sugar. He entered her stall and hesitated making eye contact. Her long eyelashes feathered over her big, dark brown eyes. Compassion welled there, and Cameron swallowed the unexpected rising emotion. "I feel the same way, Sugar."

He poured her grain then moved out of her way. Closing her stall door, he stood between them, talking to both animals. "I'm grateful the attacker didn't hurt you, but anything could've happened out there." Cameron thought of the snakes and the wildlife. He closed his eyes and offered thanks that hadn't happened. "We'll ensure protective measures so he, or she, doesn't get the chance."

His boots thudded on the creaking floorboards, and he remembered he wore no socks. Cameron chuckled to himself as he tidied the area, replacing the horse's brushes and assorted items in the tack room.

"I'll be back in a little bit to let you out," he explained to them.

After tugging open the door, he exited the stables and breathed in the fresh air. Strolling back to his cabin, he paused to study Cabin One, the closest to being finished. He smiled, recalling the silly moment of singing with Gracie and Zach.

Indignation overrode his depression. His tireless efforts to cultivate the ranch would be stripped from his hands. Gracie hadn't yet dropped the relocation bomb, but Cameron had lived long enough in WITSEC to know a safehouse was the first step to moving him. He'd lose everything because of an unidentified assailant. Would his life always be plagued running away from people trying to kill him?

Cameron returned to the stable, intending to check their water trough. Not wanting to rush through the chores, he entered the tack room and collected the thick square brush and entered Sugar's stall.

She nudged him with her nose, and he chuckled. "I didn't bring you treats, silly girl. You just finished breakfast."

He lifted the brush, then, gently touching Sugar's back, slid the coarse bristles along her reddish-brown hide.

The repetitive action soothed Cameron's thoughts, giving him time to think about Gracie.

She wasn't like anyone he'd met before. Strong and confident without an inkling of conceitedness or arrogance. If she'd been his handler from day one instead of Silas Rutherford, Cameron's view of WITSEC might've been a positive one. He grinned at the thought. Silas, for all his faults, had been an honorable man and he'd always spoken to Cameron candidly. He'd promised to never sugarcoat anything, and Silas had kept his word through to his retirement.

The thought gave him pause. Had he struggled because Silas was gone? He'd been the only constant since Cameron's parents' death.

"The bad thing about being alone with you all is too much time to ruminate," Cameron said, moving to Rocket's stall to repeat the grooming process.

Rocket nudged Cameron's outstretched arm with his bristly chin. "Don't worry, buddy. I promise to find you a good home, somebody who will take good care of you."

A rap on the door got his attention and Cameron startled.

"Cameron?" Joel's voice carried to him.

"Come on in," Cameron said, exhaling relief it wasn't the shooter. "You must have a sixth sense. Was just thinking about calling you." *And avoiding it as long as possible.*

"No kidding?" Joel entered, his boots thudding steadily on the wood floor. The man never rushed anywhere. Cameron wasn't even sure if he knew how to hurry. Joel's dark hair was hidden under a baseball cap that had seen better days. He always wore jeans and a plaid shirt. "Folks staying at your cabin said I'd find you here."

The reminder that Cameron needed to remain elusive with Zach and Gracie's identities had Cameron straightening.

"Guess who I ran into while gassing up in town?"

"I'm afraid to ask."

"She's still got it bad for you."

Cameron cringed. "Ugh."

Joel chuckled. "Let's just say Delilah is very interested in the attractive woman visiting your ranch. She mentioned something about your horses escaping and I came to check on you." He gestured toward the animals. "Apparently, she was wrong."

"Wait, Delilah knew about the horses?" Cameron's mind whirled.

"That's what she said."

Gracie was right. Delilah had been behind it. How far would Delilah go to get his attention? The possibility that she might hurt Gracie sent Cameron's teeth on edge. "How could she possibly have known that or about Gracie staying here? Don't answer that, she's already left proof of her visits."

Joel lifted a hand. "Don't shoot the messenger. I just came by to see if you needed help."

"Sorry, I've had a rough morning. Thanks for checking on me, though. We found them roaming in the park."

Joel crossed his arms over his chest and leaned against the wall. "Gracie, huh?"

"She and Zach are old friends," Cameron said, hoping they really were, so he wouldn't be lying. "They offered to help out with the renovations."

"Thought you gave your men a break to work on the cabins?" Joel asked, quirking an eyebrow.

"Yeah, I'd have to pay them," Cameron joked. "Gracie and Zach owe me from way back. Their labor doesn't fall on my payroll." No lie there.

"Say no more. I appreciate free labor and cost savings wherever possible."

"How're things at your place?" Cameron asked, fishing for information. Would Joel have the room and time to take on Sugar and Rocket?

"Good. Looking at possibly expanding if the opportunity presents itself."

"Oh, yeah? Is there land for sale around you?"

"No, but I got a couple of calls from a real estate developer interested in my property. Thinking of seeing if he'd offer me enough to buy more land elsewhere."

Cameron considered the words. Joel hadn't told him that information before. "Yeah, had the same thing. Kept telling him I wasn't interested but he was relentless. Wouldn't take no for an answer." A twinge of concern filtered through Cameron at the conversation with Gracie regarding his family's ranch. Memories of Walter Quigley's persistence returned. Had he overlooked the real estate developer?

"That's why I didn't go into sales for a career. I couldn't bug folks like that."

"Me, either." Knowing Joel was considering expanding his business alleviated Cameron's worries regarding him taking the horses. "I'll keep my ear out for any available land."

Joel shrugged. "It's not a rush or anything. You've got prime land here, my friend. Hang on to it."

Cameron swallowed hard, averting his eyes. *Yeah. I know.*

"Anyway, I'd better get a move on."

"Hey, something's come up. Any chance you could take Rocket and Sugar for me? Temporarily?" Speaking the words pained Cameron.

Joel blinked. "I'll have to make some arrangements at my stables, but I think it's doable. Can I get back to you after I get home?"

"Yes, absolutely." Cameron flicked a glance at the animals.

"Oh, almost forgot. I dropped off the package Delilah forced into my hands for you. You owe me one. She wanted to deliver it herself."

Cameron did a double take. "A package?"

"Yeah. I left it with *Gracie*." He chuckled. "I'll be in touch." Joel pushed off the wall and offered a wave.

Cameron waited until the door closed and released the horses into the pen. He opened the rear door, led them out to the pastures and perched on the side of the split rail fence, watching as they lazily grazed. Their tails swished calmly from side to side.

"Everything okay?"

Cameron twisted to see Gracie approaching with Bane. "Yeah. Joel will arrange to take Rocket and Sugar. I wasn't sure how to say I needed to move them ASAP. Didn't want to draw unnecessary attention to my departure."

"He seems like a nice guy." She leaned on the fence beside him wearing a smile that made his knees weak. "He left a package for you."

Cameron groaned. "Just throw it out. After what Joel just told me, they're probably poisoned."

"Are you kidding? The cupcakes look amazing." Gracie paused. "Wait, what?"

"Ugh." Cameron gave Gracie a recap of the conversation with his friend.

Her smile faded. "Still trying to win your affections?"

"Or poison me in the process." He grunted. "I'm not willing to test either theory."

Gracie faced the pasture. Her hair was pulled back into a ponytail, and she was wearing dark blue cargo pants with a plain tan T-shirt tucked in and a black cargo belt encircled her waist. Military-sharp and gorgeous.

"How are you feeling?" He gestured toward her leg.

"It's a little sore, but I'm good. What about you?"

"In the excitement this morning, I almost forgot about it," he admitted. "I've been focused on my reluctance at leaving this place."

"I can't imagine all you've endured." She touched his arm, and the shift was like a one-hundred-watt volt through his body. "Cam."

He faced her, mouth dry as the Badlands.

"I'm sorry about all of this. Zach and I are confident we'll find who's behind these attacks." She withdrew her touch and Cameron missed her instantly.

"Even if you do," he said, finding his voice, "it won't cancel my having to relocate again."

Gracie didn't respond, confirming his suspicions.

"There's a part of me that would prefer to surrender and hope for the best."

"Give up the fight," Gracie said.

"Exactly."

"I understand." Something in her tone made him

think she truly did. "Is there anything I can help you do here?"

"No, I'm done. Was about to head back to the cabin." He turned to face her and tried to smile but it fell flat.

"Well then, how about coffee and breakfast?"

"Sounds good."

Neither spoke as they returned to his cabin. The aroma of coffee wafted from inside and Cameron inhaled deeply.

Zach leaned against the kitchen counter and Amber was sprawled on the rug. "Good morning. I've already started the coffee."

"Tell me you didn't make it weak," Gracie replied.

"Nope."

"Should be strong enough to stand a spoon in it," Cameron replied.

"That's what I mean," Gracie replied.

Zach laughed. "You two are made for each other."

Warmth flooded Cameron at the implication that neither of them picked up on. *Shake it off.* Zach meant nothing by the comment. "I appreciate anyone who understands the right way to brew coffee," Cameron said, avoiding eye contact with Gracie.

Gracie walked to the refrigerator. "After the latest events, we need all the caffeine we can get."

Cameron smiled, withdrawing bread from the cabinet. He enjoyed spending time with her and Zach. Though he'd not admit that to them. He'd lived alone and remained aloof from acquaintances and coworkers for so long, he'd forgotten what community felt like. Cameron accepted the loneliness that came with his WITSEC existence, assuring himself it was the best way to prevent endangering anyone else. But Gracie had changed that.

"After we eat, let's put our heads together and work up a new plan," Zach said.

Like an ice-cold splash of water to the face, the comment reminded Cameron why he remained alone. The last couple of days of being attacked on his own ranch testified to the never-ending threat he faced. No matter how hard it was, the realization confirmed for Cameron that relocation was essential. He cared for his employees and wouldn't knowingly endanger them. The responsibility of helping them find new employment weighed on his shoulders. They were great and he'd not leave them high and dry.

"Amber, Bane, outside," Zach ordered. "I'll give them a quick break while you finish up here."

"Thanks," Gracie replied. When the door shut, she asked, "Cam?"

He couldn't ignore Gracie when she called him by the nickname. No one had done that, and he loved it. He fought to withhold his emotions. The truth was, he liked a lot of things Gracie did.

Too many.

She sidled up to him. "Are you okay? You seem pretty caught up in your thoughts."

"Guilty." *In ways you have no idea about.*

"Want to talk?"

"No." *Yes, and you're the first person I have wanted to open up to, but I won't.* "I'm still mulling things over in my head."

"Oh. Sure." Disappointment clouded her face, but to her credit, she didn't push him.

They worked together, moving in sync around the kitchen as though they'd known each other forever. It was easy being around her. Cameron chastised himself. He had to stop thinking about Gracie. Soon, they would part. She would go her way. He would go his. And there was a good chance they would never meet again.

Solidifying that belief, he said, "Can you tell me more about my new handler?"

"Not really. I don't know him personally. But I'm certain he will be dependable and trustworthy."

Cameron snorted.

She quirked a brow.

"Sorry. That was uncalled for. I'm a little pessimistic today. If Delilah released my horses, it doesn't explain her or the attacker knowing my real name. There has to be a mole within the marshals." Another thought landed in front of him. "What if my new handler is the mole?"

Gracie tilted her head, as though considering the option. "No. He's out of the country tending to family business from what I understand."

"Or so he says. That's an easy alibi."

"I mentioned your concerns to my boss. He was

receptive to maintaining your integrity and identity protection."

"Thanks. I appreciate that," Cameron said, meaning it. Gracie hadn't swept his concerns under the blueline-brotherhood rug without a second thought. She'd taken his comments to heart and was willing to investigate them.

The front door opened, and Zach returned with the dogs. "Whew, they needed a good run around the place to expel some energy," he said, carrying in Delilah's cupcakes. "Forgot your friend Joel left this on the porch. Already ate one. They're delicious."

Cameron and Gracie shared a concerned look.

"What?" Zach asked.

"Do you feel okay?" Cameron asked.

"Yeah, why?" Zach replied.

"Long story." Gracie offered a synopsis of what Joel had told Cameron earlier.

"Great. Well, I'm okay right now," Zach said warily.

Cameron focused on making breakfast. He didn't want to talk about his relationship ignorance with Delilah. He'd spent his whole life looking over his shoulder and within days, Gracie had shown him there were threats all around, in places he hadn't considered. And those deadly threats were closing in.

They finished the breakfast cleanup and Cameron excused himself, walking to his bedroom to pack for the safehouse.

Gracie took Bane out for a quick break, then returned to Cameron's cabin. Cameron had told them how he'd refurbished each cabin himself. She admired his handiwork. He was very talented.

She strolled through the kitchen and living area. Since Cam hadn't emerged from his bedroom, she opted to leave him alone. Her gaze traveled to the end of the counter and a large stack of papers. "Hey, Cam?"

"Yeah?" He walked out of his bedroom holding a duffel bag.

"Is there anything you need to take care of before we leave for the safehouse?" She gestured toward the stack.

"Actually, now that you mentioned it, I probably should look through that." He sorted the envelopes and papers pausing briefly to glance at a document before dropping it onto a pile. Gracie leaned closer, scanning the flyer regarding real estate development. "Is this your keep group?"

Cameron continued sorting and didn't look up. "That's trash."

"Mind if I look?"

"Nope."

Gracie lifted the paper. A gold logo at the top read Tribeca Land and Propety and promised big money for South Dakota land. "Sounds like this guy is interested in buying your ranch."

"I get those regularly. I never bother reading them." Cameron glanced at the document. "Oh, yeah. That guy was annoying as all get out."

"How so?"

"Most businesses or brokers will send a letter, make a phone call or stop by and then respectfully take the hint when I tell them no." Cameron pointed at the piece of paper. "That guy was relentless. He sent flyers daily, then called constantly. I finally had to agree to meet with him in person, hoping a face-to-face conversation would get through to him."

"And what happened?"

"He never showed up."

Gracie considered the information. "Why would someone that persistent just back off?"

"Who knows?" Cameron returned to sorting the mail. "Anyway, I wouldn't sell it off to some corporation. Not that I intended to leave this soon. Regardless, I want it to go to someone who is willing to put the heart and soul into the place like I have."

"I appreciate what you've said. However, bearing in mind the latest developments, maybe call him and see if he's interested?"

"No way. I got bad vibes off the dude." Cameron shook his head. "He was pushy and rude. Not to mention he was a no-show. That speaks to integrity."

Gracie studied the advertisement, certain she was missing something.

"I've got a few things I want to take to the safehouse," Cameron said.

"Uh-huh," Gracie answered absently, still rereading the paper.

Cameron moved next to her. "What are you so intrigued with?"

"I'm not sure." Gracie lifted her eyes, meeting Cameron's curious gaze. "You said he was super pushy?"

"Yep, took it to a whole new level. Then skips out on the meeting without as much as a phone call. Beyond inconsiderate after the effort he made to set the appointment in the first place."

Gracie tilted her head. "You don't find that strange?"

"I was relieved. I didn't care enough to follow up. Just figured the guy finally took the hint or found better property."

No. That didn't jibe. Why would someone work to meet with Cameron then not show up? "Do you think any of your employees spoke to him?"

Cameron crossed his arms over his chest. "You're hung up on this."

"I'm just working through the information."

"Kent McCarthy and Foster Esparza are my best workers. They understand my philosophies and priorities. Kent was in the office the day I agreed to meet with the dude on the phone. Hmm, can't even remember his name. Anyway, he knew I was furious."

"They're protective of you."

"I wouldn't say that, but they've got my back. Kent and Foster are great guys." Cameron glanced down.

"There's no names listed."

"I think he said John."

Zach returned.

"Hey, perfect timing." Gracie waved him over and updated Zach.

"I'd say it's worth digging into," he agreed.

"He's just an obnoxious salesman," Cameron said. "Though it does bring back memories of Walter Quigley's actions with my parents."

Gracie withdrew her cell phone. "Let's involve Cheyenne's skills and see what she finds out."

"If nothing else, maybe details about the owner," Zach suggested.

Gracie made the call, placing it on speakerphone.

"Hey, guys, what's up?" Cheyenne answered.

"In all your spare time, would you be willing to help us with one more thing?" Gracie asked.

Cheyenne laughed. "Of course."

"Check out this Tribeca Land and Property," Gracie said.

"Okay, looking for anything in particular?"

"Financials, owners names, location," Gracie responded. "All we have is a post-office box."

"Add in any connections, financial holdings, et cetera," Zach added.

"On it, I'll be in touch," Cheyenne replied, disconnecting.

"Financial trails have destroyed famous criminals in the past. You'd be surprised what the coup de grâce is that results in their demise," Gracie said.

"Whoever is after you is relentless, and we need to understand their motive."

"Other than wanting me dead," Cameron said. "Walter Quigley has always been suspect number one. And Phillip's real estate company focused on luxury vacation homes in California. That's a far cry from a South Dakota ranch." Cameron pinched his forehead. "I'm tired of this fight and of running."

Gracie wanted to reach out and assure him that things would get better, but she couldn't. For professional and personal reasons. "I still think any connections to Quigley, like Phillip, Imogene and Noonan, are our best sources, but we won't rule out ones that are less obvious." Gracie couldn't shake the feeling that the real estate developer was involved. The connection was too strong. "Did this guy appear angry?"

Cameron shook his head. "No, he was the typical salesman. 'How about if I call you in a couple of days when you've had time to think about it.' That kind of guy."

"Would you mind contacting Kent and Foster to see if they spoke with him?" Gracie asked.

"Sure." Cameron withdrew his cell phone, placing the call. "Hey, Kent. Am I catching you at a bad time?" A pause. "Great. Do you remember that real estate dude who wouldn't take a hint?" Cameron smiled and laughed. "Yep, that's the one. Did you ever talk to him?"

Gracie kept her eyes on him.

"Yeah, no. Just wondering. Dude never showed up or apologized… Right? Okay… No, I'm still working on the cabins. There's so much to do... No, take the time off. You've earned it. Thanks." Cameron hung up. "Kent never spoke to the guy, but he remembered his last name was Hogue."

"Excellent," Gracie said, updating Cheyenne via text. She also asked Cheyenne to check into Cameron's employees, Foster and Kent.

Cameron repeated the process with Foster. "You did?" Cameron shot Gracie a quizzical glance. "And?... Hmm. Interesting... I don't remember you mentioning this before." Another long pause. "No, man, it's all good. Thanks." He disconnected. "Foster said he caught the guy lurking around the back side of the ranch, and he acted all squirrely."

"Casing the property?" Gracie mused.

"Sounds like it," Zach said. "Why didn't he tell you this before?"

"I asked the same thing. He apologized. Said he was having a rotten day at that time and thought he told me."

Gracie and Zach shared a look that said they didn't buy it.

"Let's talk out what we know for sure. This Hogue guy is interested in the property and wants to buy it so bad then when he finally gets the opportunity to talk to you face-to-face, he doesn't show up?" Gracie tapped her fingers on the counter. "That makes no sense."

Cameron paced a small area near her, deep in thought. After several seconds, he said, "If he was casing my land, did he see something that made him reconsider buying it?"

"Hmm." Zach met her gaze. "Now that's an interesting take."

"What would make it undesirable to a buyer?" Gracie asked. "You said he interacted with Foster?"

"Only when Foster caught him lurking."

"Which he failed to mention to you," Zach inserted. "When did you start the renovations on the cabins?"

Cameron walked to the stack of papers he'd sorted through earlier and withdrew a calendar. "About a month ago."

"Establishing a timeline," Zach said. "When did the guy first contact you?"

"Easily six months before that," Cameron replied.

"Was Hogue cold-calling landowners or did something draw him here?" Gracie asked.

"Could be—" Zach began.

"Hmm, now that you mention it, Delilah helps promote the local businesses as a side hustle. Without my approval, she featured Pronghorn Hills Guest Ranch in a publication prior to Hogue's incessant phone calls and letters."

"That explains what drew him here." Gracie nodded. "What suddenly changed? Was that before or after you and Delilah first dated?"

Cameron shot a quick glance at Zach and Gracie realized she'd exposed his secret, but they had to consider every piece of evidence regardless of emotions.

"Is there something on the ranch this Hogue dude wants? If it was the land, you'd think he would've followed through on the meeting," Zach asked.

"I think the answer to all of this hinges on who Hogue is." Gracie glanced at her cell phone, willing it to ring with an update. This was it, the clue they needed. "Come on, Cheyenne. Fill in the missing link."

ELEVEN

Cameron walked outside and slid onto a chair on the porch. All their talk of suspects solidified what he already believed—he was a human destruction magnet. Nobody would be safe with him.

The door opened and Gracie emerged. "Mind if I join you?"

"I was hoping for a little alone time."

"I understand, but that's not safe," Gracie replied.

Cameron stifled his frustration. "Sure." Except time with Gracie was exactly what he was avoiding. He pushed himself out of the chair. "Shall we?"

They headed out, Bane trotting off leash with them.

"Why did you name the place Pronghorn Hills Guest Ranch? Are there a lot of them wandering around the property?"

He appreciated the change in subject—he never tired of talking about his ranch. "No. I saw one the day I purchased the property and it seemed fitting." Cameron sighed. "There are a lot of them in Wyoming. Seeing the pronghorn here reminded me of my home and solidified my reason for staying here."

"That makes a lot of sense," Gracie said. "When I couldn't sleep last night, I did a little online research about pronghorns. They're fascinating creatures. Did you know they can run up to sixty miles an hour, making them the second fastest animal in the world?"

Great, he was so boring, he'd forced Gracie into a conversation about wildlife. And yet, Cameron hated that he craved her company. He also recognized her efforts to take his mind off the current situation. When he didn't reply, Gracie continued. "The first fastest is the cheetah, but the pronghorn can maintain the speed for a longer period of time."

Cameron tried to think of something intelligent to say. "Hmm." *That's the best you've got? Ugh.*

"Here's another fun fact," Gracie rambled, either oblivious to his uncomfortableness or ignoring it. "Herds of pronghorns migrate up to one hundred and fifty miles each way. Only caribous have that similar trait."

Cameron guffawed, unable to stop himself.

Gracie stopped. "What?"

"Just thinking of the ironic facts. I named this place after an animal known for migrating from place to place, and the creature must do it fast. A perfect picture of my life."

Gracie smiled. "I suppose that's true enough."

Cameron walked to a picnic area centered under a tree between two of the cabins and perched on the tabletop, keeping one leg on the bench. "I hate being forced off my land."

"One of the things the marshals did when our family went into protective custody was promise to always be honest with us. I appreciated that. We'd been through so much and I didn't want them lying to us or pretending." Gracie moved closer but remained standing. "I assure you I will also be honest with you."

Cameron nodded, unsure where she was going with the conversation.

"I wish I could tell you that it will all work out. But you've already seen the brutality of criminals."

"Yeah," Cameron grunted.

"It doesn't give them the final say in your life."

Cameron looked past her into the beauty of the landscape beyond Gracie. "Feels like the bad guys keep winning and I'm forced to accept defeat."

"That's all attitude."

Cameron whipped his head around to face her. "What's that supposed to mean?" His tone was harsher than he intended, but it felt like a smack to be told he was wimping out.

"You see yourself as overcome in the battle. I see you fighting for your life and for what's right. Totally different perspectives."

Cameron's defensiveness evaporated. "I appreciate having a say in my life. You included me in the case. It's empowering." He rested his hands on his knees. "I can't imagine not owning a ranch. It's the closest I've felt to having a real home since entering WITSEC."

Compassion, not pity, flooded Gracie's green irises. "Have you requested career options?"

"Not really. I've accepted wherever they assign me. Guess I hadn't considered voicing an opinion."

She shrugged. "Might be worth inquiring. Since I don't work in WITSEC, I can't offer an intelligent answer, but as my dad would say, it's free to ask."

For the first time, Cameron had an inkling of hope for his future. He'd acquiesced to go and be whatever the marshals instructed, and he'd not entertained other options. Gracie made him braver than he'd ever felt before. She made him want to hope and strive toward a future. She made him want to be a better man. And he dared not tell her any of that.

His gaze traveled the contours of her face, lingering on her lips. Her inward beauty enhanced her already attractive features. Their eyes held for several seconds. She enveloped him with her green irises.

"You're an amazing woman, Gracie."

"Thank you." She smiled. "No one's ever said that to me before."

"They missed the opportunity." Warmth filled Cameron's chest and he couldn't stop admiring her. He reached for her hand. "Thank you for sticking with me, even though you're not a WITSEC handler. I appreciate everything."

"I've enjoyed getting to know you."

They remained close, her hand in his. Cameron's

heart drummed hard with anticipation. He wanted to tell her the truth, but words eluded him. Before he thought twice, he found himself leaning closer. Gracie met him in the middle, and their lips brushed softly.

Her cell phone rang, interrupting them.

Gracie jerked back and blinked. Cameron looked down at his boots. What had he done? He had no right to compromise her job.

"It's Cheyenne," Gracie said, taking a step backward.

Cameron understood the distancing. She was out of his league, and completely off-limits. He'd overstepped their professional boundaries. The faster he got that through his delusional imagination, the better for them both.

"Let's see what Cheyenne found." She answered the phone, placing it on speakerphone. "Hey, got anything good to share?"

"Did I catch you at a bad time?" Cheyenne asked.

Gracie chuckled, and Cameron picked up on the nervousness in her tone. "Not at all."

No, you saved us from making a terrible mistake.

"Oh, good. So listen to this. Imogene Yarborough, that was Walter Quigley's significant other," Cheyenne said as though Cameron needed a reminder, "remarried and changed her name."

"After Quigley's mess went public, she probably wanted to distance herself and a name change provided that escape," Gracie replied.

"Agreed. Imogene's, aka Amelia's, last name

is what you're going to be interested in." Cheyenne paused. "Her new husband's name is Hillard Hogue, and they own a real-estate-development company."

Gracie and Cameron remained frozen in place.

"No wonder we couldn't find anything on her," Gracie replied.

"Yep, and there's more," Cheyenne said. "Hogue was Walter Quigley's business partner before he got into politics. Hillard passed away leaving Imogene, aka Amelia, a significant amount of money, which she squandered. Then she filed bankruptcy and closed the business."

"There's our connection," Cameron said.

"Right," Cheyenne agreed.

"Great work," Gracie replied.

"One additional interesting fact is the CFO for Tribeca Land and Property is John Vindicta."

"Should that mean something to me?" Cameron asked.

"Did you say Vindicta?" Gracie queried.

Cameron met her gaze. "What're you thinking?"

"Spell it for me," Gracie asked.

Cheyenne did as she asked. "It's unusual."

"Hmm, thanks, Cheyenne. We'll head to the cabin and include Zach, then call you back."

"Yeah, you'll want to hear the rest of this," Cheyenne said. "I'll be here."

They disconnected.

"Am I missing something?"

"I don't know yet." Gracie whistled for Bane, and he returned immediately.

Cameron struggled to keep up with Gracie as they hurried back to his cabin. Zach was waiting on the porch while Amber strolled the yard. "We've got an update." Gracie waved him inside.

She withdrew her laptop and sat at the table, tapping the keys in lightning-fast speed. "I knew it."

Cameron and Zach exchanged a look.

Cameron shrugged and said, "I'm on the edge of my seat."

"I wanted to verify my suspicions before I said anything." Gracie looked up from her computer. "The name bugged me because it was familiar. Vindicta is Latin for revenge."

Cameron blinked. "My attacker's name is John Revenge?"

"It's a pseudonym," Gracie said. "Let's include Cheyenne." She dialed the number while Zach and Cameron remained confused.

"Okay, we're all here and you're on speakerphone," Gracie said. "What's the rest you discovered?"

"John Vindicta left Tribeca after allegations of fraud and money laundering were made. They tried to keep it on the downlow in an agreement deal, but nothing is buried for good if there's a paper trail," Cheyenne replied. "And here's where things get weird. Imogene, aka Amelia, was supposed to meet with the prosecutor regarding the case, then she suddenly went missing several months ago. The police have a missing-persons report and John was considered a person of interest for a while, but was recently cleared."

"She's still missing?" Zach asked.

"Yes," Cheyenne replied. "There's nothing solid to indicate foul play and it's not totally unheard of for a woman of means to take off. Imogene reinvented herself once, so she could've done it again."

"But why?" Gracie asked.

"Good question," Cheyenne said. "I'm still digging into this John Vindicta's identity, but the guy is a ghost. As of now, that's all I know."

"Outstanding work," Gracie replied.

They disconnected and she faced Cameron with a look of triumph. "Are you thinking what I am?"

"John was interested in buying your land until he got fired," Zach surmised.

"Sounds like it," Cameron agreed. "And apparently Imogene, aka Amelia, was either in on the money laundering or about to rat him out."

"That's my take. She's either a partner or he took her out to keep her quiet. We need to know who the mysterious John Vindicta is. And was he impersonating Hillard Hogue? If so, why?"

Too many questions complicated Cameron's life. Hadn't Gracie said revenge was a substantial criminal motive? A man who dubbed himself Mr. Revenge, linked to his past explained how he'd known Cameron's real name. The answers didn't alleviate his fears about fighting a faceless assailant who'd studied Cameron. He flicked a glance at Gracie, busy talking with Zach. Worse, Cameron's instincts said the criminal would do anything to finish him off. Including targeting Gracie.

The sun had settled low in the sky by the time Gracie helped Cameron finish packing up the necessary supplies. As they waited for his friend Joel to arrive, they strolled near the stables, where the horses were ready to load into his trailer.

"I hate inventing a reason for Joel to take them," Cameron said.

"I know," Gracie assured him. "What did you say?"

"An unexpected family obligation required me to go out of town." Cameron entered the stables and Gracie followed.

"How well do you know Joel?"

He moved toward the back, where a small sign read *tack room*, and entered. Inside, saddles, blankets, harnesses and other buckets and containers filled the space. She leaned against the wall, watching as he maneuvered around, organizing the objects.

"Joel's a good guy. For obvious reasons I'm not especially close to anyone, so he doesn't know a lot about my 'life,'" he explained. "But he's the only one I'd trust to take my animals."

"That says a lot," Gracie replied.

Cameron exhaled a long breath. "After living on a superficial level with anyone I'm around, I sometimes wonder if I'm capable of an in-depth relationship." His eyes met hers. "You're the first person I've openly confided in. I'd forgotten how much I missed the freedom to do that."

Gracie nodded, unsure how to respond.

The sound of a large diesel engine interrupted their conversation, and they exited the tack room and stables. The large pickup pulled onto the property, and they moved to allow Joel to park.

"I appreciate this," Cameron greeted Joel as he exited the truck.

"Not a problem. Happy to help. Who knows I might be calling on you someday for a return favor," Joel said, slapping him on the back.

Cameron and Gracie shared a knowing glance and sadness for Cameron's circumstances hovered over her like a cloud. Unless something changed, Cameron would be in the wind by then. Cameron frowned and his demeanor reverted to his earlier melancholy mood.

"Unsure how long you'll be?" Joel asked.

Cameron looked at Gracie for support.

"You know how it is with family obligations," Gracie inserted. "It's impossible to estimate a date."

"Not a problem. Rest assured, your horses are in good hands. I had an increase in riding tours, so it actually helps me," Joel said.

Gracie's interest piqued and she studied Joel. He had a need for the horses, and with Cameron's situation, he'd acquired two trained animals for free. He had motive to hurt Cameron. Why hadn't they looked closer at Joel? She made a mental note to follow up as soon as possible.

"Yeah, the last few days have been full of surprises," Cameron continued, oblivious to her thoughts. "Again, just grateful you were able to take them while I deal with this."

"Well, let's get 'em loaded," Joel replied.

Gracie moved back while Cameron and Joel worked with obvious experience to transfer the animals into the back of the trailer. Cameron's strong but gentle mannerisms with the majestic creatures spoke to his character. He was both of those things. If only they could find the assassin and allow Cameron to return to the life he'd worked to build here. Yet, for all Gracie's optimism, she knew the possibility was slim. She'd not give him false hope.

Cameron closed the gate of the horse trailer, and the men shook hands.

"Pleasure meeting you. Next time I hope we can extend the visit." Joel offered a tip of his hat to Gracie.

"Absolutely." The reply slipped off her lips before she realized what she'd said.

Joel slid behind the wheel of his diesel pickup and slowly departed through the gates of the property.

"I hate being a contributor to the destruction of your dreams," Gracie said.

"I don't hold anything against you. You're following orders just like me," Cameron replied, a softness in his eyes. "I appreciate your understanding."

They started to stroll to the cabin. "Until I met you, I don't think I grasped how unfair it is for our agency to ask a person to never have a future or stability for the rest of their life while they remained in Witness Protection," Gracie replied. "The program was developed to be a positive assistance to those in need."

"Yeah, and it keeps me from dying at the hands of another. I'm grateful. I just wish this would end."

Gracie's cell phone rang and she withdrew the device from her pocket. Brafford's contact information appeared on the screen, and she frowned. Instinct said something wasn't right. He rarely contacted her first. Dreading the call already, she swiped to answer, placing the phone against her ear. "Fitzgerald."

"Gracie, are you still at the Pronghorn Ranch?"

"Yes, sir."

"Good. I'm glad I caught you in time. We've got a problem."

"I wish that surprised me," Gracie replied.

"The safehouse we planned for you to take Cameron to was compromised in another case. We just found out that the witness who had stayed there a while back shared the location to another contact. It's unsafe for you to travel there now."

"No," Gracie breathed. "Sir, all due respect, we're not sure it's safe for us to remain here, either."

"Any further attacks?" he asked.

"Negative. And we just transferred Cameron's horses off the ranch."

"Hmm… Who's aware you're leaving?"

"Only Cameron's friend who took the horses. Keystone Deputy Zach Kelcey from DGTF is here with me."

"That's a positive. Can the two of you handle Cameron's protective duty until I can get you another location?"

"Yes."

"Thanks, Gracie. I'll be in touch ASAP."

They disconnected and the worry etched on Cameron's face said he'd discerned there was an issue from the discussion.

Gracie relayed the details, confused by the relief that washed over Cameron's expression. "One more night to stay on my property? I'll take that as a win."

"You never cease to surprise me," Gracie said, feeling relieved, too. "We need to update Zach." She led the way to the cabin.

Zach stood beside his unit. "What's up?"

"We've got a delay." She repeated the information regarding the safehouse.

"Hurry up and wait. It's the government way," Zach said. "Okay, we'll just keep watch. At least the horses are safe, and we don't have to worry about them."

"I don't sleep much anymore, I can take first watch," Cameron said.

"Negative," Gracie said, then held up her hand. Not wanting to offend Cameron, she said, "If my boss learned I snoozed while you kept watch, I'd face his wrath."

"Can't put you in your superior's crosshairs," Cameron replied good-naturedly. "I'll take one for the team."

Gracie chuckled. "Zach, let's secure the perimeter and then I'll take first watch." Once they were alone performing the check, she said, "I could be totally off base, but I'm reconsidering Joel Iverson as a suspect. He mentioned expanding his ranch and needing more horses. He'd also told Cameron he was envious of the property here."

"He stands to benefit from Cameron selling it," Zach surmised.

"Right, and what if Imogene's interest is peripheral and not direct? She could be Joel's agent."

Zach listened but offered no additional information. "Hm. Let's head back and talk to Cameron."

By the time they finished the reconnaissance, night was descending on the area. Settled inside the cabin, Zach mentioned Gracie's suspicions with Cameron.

"Joel's ranch offers comparable services to mine," Cameron agreed. "And he's mentioned more than once how much he likes my property."

"How well does he know it?" Gracie asked.

Cameron considered the question. "As much as my employees. He's helped with odd jobs around here before."

"And he'd know where to park while casing the property, the times he shot up the cabins, as well as attacking Gracie at the start," Cameron added and groaned. "And I just gave him my horses."

"Are you worried he'll hurt them?" Zach asked.

"No. Not at all. And doing so wouldn't benefit him. He needs them for his ranch." Cameron hesitated, then said, "He also mentioned receiving offers from real estate agents for his ranch too."

"Legit or trying to throw us off?" Gracie asked.

They spent the remainder of the evening talking through the facts. The biggest hindrance was figuring out how John Vindicta and Joel Iverson were connected. Joel was no real-estate executive. Their deep search into the man's history provided no further leads. He'd established a guest ranch very similar to Cameron's a year prior to Pronghorn Hills opening. But Joel was on the northern side and Cameron had the better ground. Had he befriended Cameron hoping to buy the land? And if so, why send in John? Too many disconnects made the situation difficult to figure out.

Gracie took the first watch while the men retreated to their respective rooms to rest. She sat near the partially open living room window, where she had a good view of the gate and entrance.

Crickets chirped in the background and the serenity of the night settled. Fresh air wafted in, carrying the scent of pine. She stretched out her legs and leaned back in the chair. Bane strolled to her side, his nails clicking on the hardwood floor. He sat beside her, and she absently stroked his velvety ears. "Lord, this puzzle is complicated and we're missing a major piece. I don't know how You will work this all together, but I know that You will somehow. You have a plan for Cameron's life. And maybe part of this is to bring him back to You."

She closed her eyes, awakened by Bane's growl.

Gracie jolted upright and glanced at the clock on her phone. She gave herself a mental thwack. She'd fallen asleep! Her gaze reverted to Bane, who stood, hackles raised, facing the door. Gracie withdrew her gun from the leg holster and slowly slid out of the chair, staying low and moving flat against the wall.

She peered through the side window without compromising her safe place, searching for any movement. Her ears perked for any sounds.

Nothing.

Gracie's gaze searched the cabin. Cameron and Zach's bedrooms were at the far side. She didn't want to alert them and have them walk right into danger. Without knowing what she faced, Gracie held her place, all senses on high alert.

Bane's posture remained guarded, his gaze fixed on the front door. The guttural warning growl rumbled in the Malinois' chest.

Someone was outside the cabin.

TWELVE

Gracie typed Intruder into her cell phone and sent it to Zach. She slid from the recliner, melting silently to the floor and crawling to the wall beside the front door. There, she flattened herself out of sight, tightly gripping her duty weapon.

"Bane, back," she whisper-hissed.

The Malinois flicked a glance at her as though trying to talk her out of the order. She offered a hand signal, reinforcing her words, and Bane backed away slowly.

"Down."

He dropped flat and she lifted her hand in the command to stay.

To reach the hallway where Cameron and Zach slept, she had to cross the room, exposed.

Gracie surveyed the open concept cabin, where a single table lamp provided light. She continued her examination, checking that the window blinds were closed, preventing whoever was outside from seeing her before she dared to move to the hallway. As her reconnaissance returned to the place where she'd sat only moments before, Gracie sucked in a breath. There was a two-inch gap in the blinds, reminding her she'd opened the window earlier.

Gracie stayed low, creeping toward the hallway, directly across from the front door. The two spare rooms were opposite Cameron's room and the bathroom. She had to warn Zach and Cameron before they stepped out.

The sound of shuffling behind Zach's closed door had Gracie freezing in place. It cracked open and Gracie waved him down. With Amber at his side, he squatted. She pointed toward Bane, who remained focused on the entrance, hackles raised.

Zach bolted across the hallway and opened Cameron's door, disappearing inside.

Gracie got Bane's attention and gave him hand signals to crawl to her. He obeyed, silently closing the distance.

Zach and Cameron emerged, and the group made their way behind the kitchen counter, which separated the rooms. The elongated rectangular cabinet provided breakfast bar eating space and sat centered, concealing them while offering the best visual of the living area. Zach and Gracie took opposite sides, crouched and peered around each side of the massive island.

Silence hovered like a ticking bomb.

Had the intruder left?

No one dared to move.

A click got their attention.

Automatic gunfire erupted, pelting the walls and

shattering windows in a relentless attack, precluding them from returning fire.

Gracie, Cameron and Zach stayed down, covering their heads with their arms and shielding the dogs between them.

They had nowhere to run where they'd be protected from flying bullets.

Fleeing to the bedrooms wasn't an option, either.

Vulnerable and trapped in place while the gunshots rained down on them like a war zone, the trio waited anxiously for a reprieve.

Gracie and Zach positioned their weapons, prepared to return fire.

The front door blasted open, and the shooter emerged, sweeping the automatic gun from right to left, spraying the room with bullets.

Gracie twisted to see Zach was no longer behind her. He must've crept to the other side of the island. Their only hope of survival was conducting multiple attacks.

She met Cameron's terrified stare. "Stay down," she whispered, then shifted to a prone position and peered around the corner enough to gauge the shooter's location.

The man stood at least four feet away, and from her vantage point, she struggled to see his face. Gracie fired.

He hollered, finger still on the trigger, and sprayed gunfire across the floorboards.

In her peripheral vision, Zach appeared from the opposite side of the island and lunged for the man.

He tackled the intruder, forcing his gun from his hand. The weapon tumbled to the ground with a thud.

The two engaged in fierce combat, punching, kicking and rolling around the hardwood floor.

Gracie pounced on the gun—an AK-47. She snagged it, holding it against her body, and scurried away from where Zach and the intruder continued fighting.

Cameron was at her side immediately, and she passed him the weapon. "Hold this and get down!"

No way was she leaving the gun anywhere the shooter might snatch it again.

Cameron moved behind the island, cradling the massive firearm.

Gracie aimed, struggling for a clear shot that didn't endanger Zach, but the erratic fighting maneuvers of the combatants made it nearly impossible.

The fight grew more intense with neither showing any indication of surrendering.

"Get up!" Gracie ordered, holding her gun on the shooter and Zach. They ignored her and she fired a warning shot into the ceiling.

The distraction worked for a second, allowing Zach to plunge his fist into the intruder's gut.

The man stumbled backward, but Zach delivered the final uppercut, dropping him to his knees. Zach jerked the intruder upright.

He reluctantly complied, his massive frame heaving from the exertion. He fixed a murderous glare at Gracie. She kept her gun trained on him, undeterred. “Move and I’ll shoot,” she warned.

“Cameron, grab my handcuffs on the nightstand,” Zach ordered.

“Yes, *James*, be a good little witness and do what you’re told,” the man said in a mocking tone.

“Phillip Quigley.” Cameron exited the kitchen, still carrying the AK-47.

Gracie did a double take as recognition hit her. Time and hatred had aged Phillip significantly.

Cameron stormed toward Phillip, fury in every step. “Why after all these years?”

“You ruined my life! James, you’re nothing more than a plague.”

“I was a kid and I haven’t even seen you in twelve years!” Cameron contended.

“How’d you find him?” Gracie asked.

“Imogene’s brilliant work. Imagine my surprise when I discovered my enemy owned the prime real estate I wanted.” Phillip pinned her with a dark glare. “I stopped by to inquire about the ranch, and the moment I saw James parading around the land the government gave him. Gave him!” he screeched, straining against Zach’s hold. “—I knew I’d finally have the chance to exact my revenge.”

“You’re John Vindicta,” Zach surmised.

“Yes.” Phillip’s reptilian smile widened. “You’re harder to kill than I expected. Not for lack of trying, though. The bunker was intriguing. Useless, but you get an A for effort.”

“That’s enough,” Zach warned.

"No," Cameron replied. "Let him talk. I want to know everything."

"You stalked him," Gracie pressed.

"Hunted," Phillip corrected. "After all, he sent my dad to prison and destroyed my life."

"Walter Quigley killed my parents," Cameron blurted.

Phillip offered a slight shrug. "Guess we see things differently."

"How were Imogene and Delilah involved?" Zach asked.

"Imogene inherited her husband's money and after pretending to care for me, I figured she owed me. She disagreed." Phillip grunted. "Stupid cow! She lied to the cops, claiming I threatened her…please!"

"So you killed her?" Gracie asked.

"Is she dead? Last I heard she was missing." Phillip grinned. "Maybe she ran away or got mixed up with the wrong people."

Gracie shook her head. "What about Delilah or Arlcc?"

"Who?" Phillip seemed genuinely confused. "No clue who you're talking about."

"It's over," Cameron said.

Phillip guffawed. "Ya think it's that easy? Danger's unpredictable. I'd watch your back, James. Never know what's coming. In fact, Dad's up for parole soon. He's many years to contemplate his hatred of you. As have his loyal constituents. And money is a powerful incentive. Thanks to Imogene, there's no lack of that supply."

"Are you threatening him?" Gracie demanded.

"Just laying out the facts. You might've stopped me, but you can't stop everyone. The workers are plentiful." He guffawed.

"He's lying," Gracie said.

"Am I?" Phillip countered.

"Is there a mole in the marshals?" Cameron asked.

Phillip laughed again. "Idiot. You think I got a map with your location? I don't need insider knowledge. You can't hide from my family, James. We'll always find you."

Grateful to hear there wasn't a mole in the marshals helping Phillip, Gracie said, "Cam, ignore him. Grab the cuffs." She stepped between the men.

Cameron narrowed his eyes, then silently exited the room to do as she asked. Gracie turned just as Phillip spun, thrusting his elbow into Zach's face, and slammed him against the wall. A sickening snap corresponded with Zach's holler of pain. Phillip lunged at her.

"Bane, *fass*!" Gracie ordered, using the German command to attack.

Her dog sprang from his crouched position beside her, and the fur missile launched into the air, clamping his razor-sharp teeth with perfect precision onto the shooter's left forearm, eliciting a scream. Phillip spun in a circle, taking Bane with him.

The Malinois clung tight, refusing to release his hold.

"Get off me!" Phillip screeched.

"My dog won't let go until you stop moving," Gracie said.

He ignored her, struggling fruitlessly against Bane's powerful bite. The dog hung from his left forearm with determination.

Her gaze flicked to Zach, who was gripping his right shoulder in pain. He shifted, revealing his arm hung at an awkward angle. The jerk had dislocated it when he'd slammed Zach into the wall. The injury incapacitated Zach's firing hand. He moved back, distancing himself from the intruder.

Gracie focused on Phillip, who was engaged in full battle with Bane. His beefy hand disappeared into the leather jacket pocket.

Light bounced off the metal.

Gracie's eyes widened. "Gun!"

In what felt like horribly slow motion, Gracie saw Phillip position the barrel at Bane.

"Bane, off!" Gracie screamed. "Off!"

The dog released and sprang to her side, narrowly avoiding the bullet fired in his direction. In the brief second, she'd averted her gaze, Phillip aimed his pistol on Gracie.

Rapid shots exploded.

Phillip's eyes widened in surprise, his gun still in hand. He fell backward.

Gracie and Zach exchanged confused looks. Neither had shot their weapons. Gracie pivoted to see Cameron holding Phillip's AK-47.

* * *

Cameron stood dazed. He'd never wielded a weapon with such incredible firepower, and he'd not expected to release that many rounds in rapid succession. His heart thrummed with vicious force against his ribs, and he scarcely heard Gracie until she moved in front of him. "Cam! Are you okay?"

He blinked, his mouth dry, and croaked, "It just happened."

"You saved my life." She gently took the gun from him and set it on the counter.

His hands burned—whether from the experience or adrenaline, he wasn't certain.

Cameron swallowed and nodded, struggling to speak.

"It's all right, man. Breathe." Zach approached, his face contorted in pain. His left hand clutched his right shoulder and his arm hung awkwardly.

Dislocated. Cameron had experienced the horrible effects of that injury and knew firsthand about the excruciating agony.

"We need to get you to a hospital," Gracie said, reaching for her phone.

"It's only dislocated," Zach groaned between clenched teeth, confirming Cameron's silent assessment. "I'm not going to the hospital. Besides, we've got to deal with him." He gestured at Phillip with the fingers of his good hand.

"I'll notify Daniel and Brafford." Gracie spoke into her phone and Zach faced Cameron.

"You okay, dude?" Zach's inquiry echoed as

though spoken through a tunnel. When Cameron didn't respond, Zach repeated, "Cameron, are you all right?"

Forcing himself to engage, Cameron mumbled, "I don't know. I've never killed anyone."

"If you hadn't shot him, he would've killed Gracie."

"I reacted, and I didn't realize—" His gaze moved to where the AK-47 sat on the countertop. "He aimed at Gracie and—"

"And you saved my life," Gracie reassured him, touching his arm.

"It was Phillip Quigley all along."

"Appears so," Gracie said. "Come sit down, both of you."

"Negative, I need to walk," Zach grumbled, moving toward the kitchen.

Gracie ushered Cameron to the sofa, where he perched on the edge of the cushion. She returned to Phillip and reached for the man's wallet, peeking out from his back pocket. She withdrew a card, studied it for a minute, then handed it to Cameron. *Tribeca Land and Property, John Vindicta* was written in thick gold lettering on the navy business card and his picture was printed in color on the bottom right side.

"Foster met Phillip aka John Vindicta."

"I'll have Foster brought in for questioning and hopefully he'll identify Phillip as the man he talked to."

A loud thud and grunt behind them got their attention. Zach massaged his shoulder. "See? Just needed to slam it back into place."

"I can't even," Gracie replied, shaking her head.

Zach chuckled and took the dogs outside, leaving them alone.

"My boss, Supervisory Deputy US Marshal Brafford, has ordered us to report to him first thing in the morning to discuss next steps."

Cameron hung his head. "This nightmare will never end."

"I'm sorry. But I'll be right beside you." Gracie touched his hand.

"Thank you." He'd faced all his trials alone. Knowing Gracie would stay with him provided a measure of support. Even if it was temporary. He lifted his eyes, meeting hers.

"I came close to dying tonight and didn't know it until it was too late. Funny thing is it made me realize what I really want in this stage of my life."

"What's that?"

"My career has been my safety net from the world and pain. But it hasn't changed the fact that I'm ready for a future outside of my job."

"What's that look like?"

"Marriage and children. Coming home to the same place every night not living out of a duffel bag on assignment."

Cameron averted his eyes. "Guess I gave up any hope of that happening in my life."

Gracie opened her mouth then closed it again. "Sorry. Totally bad timing on my part."

"No. I'm glad you're comfortable telling me." Cameron meant the words.

"Anyway, I've also requested Joel and Delilah come in for questioning," Gracie said, diverting topics.

"Why?"

"I've got questions that need answers," Gracie replied cryptically.

Unable to argue for lack of energy, he nodded.

"We'll meet he and Foster at the local PD in the morning. You'll be permitted to watch the interrogation."

His gaze returned to where Phillip was lying, and Cameron's stomach roiled. The threat had finally been eliminated, and yet he had no idea what the future held. Despite everything, his whole life was possibly about to change.

Cameron walked out to Gracie's patrol unit, leaving the Plains City PD and heading to the US Marshal headquarters. Relief mingled with sadness. Foster had positively identified Phillip, confirming he'd cased the ranch for some time. He targeted Cameron after the combination of getting fired and dumped triggered his hunger for revenge.

After interviewing Delilah, they determined she was a nuisance but not involved with Phillip. Joel, his friend, had been cleared too. He'd entrusted Joel to care for Rocket and Sugar and couldn't bear the thought that he'd handed them over to a conspirator to murder. Cameron buckled up, and Bane shifted in his kennel, allowing Cameron to scratch him behind the ears.

The drive was solemn and by the time Gracie pulled up to the large building, Cameron was beyond exhausted. But they had unfinished business to attend to, and he needed to know where he'd go from here.

"Are you ready for this?" Gracie asked.

"Not really," Cameron replied. "Will I face charges for killing Phillip?"

"Absolutely not. That was self-defense. Zach and I are both witnesses to everything."

"Good. Considering I had no other choice. Short of running away?" He laughed bitterly.

"It'll all work out," she assured him.

Cameron snorted. "Yeah." He made no effort to hide his frustration. Even with Phillip dead, he expected he'd remain in WITSEC. He'd never be free.

They exited the vehicle and Gracie released Bane, snapping on his leash. With the exuberance of a zombie, Cameron trailed behind Gracie. They entered the nondescript brick building, where the sterile environment offered no comfort. The elevator didn't even play bad music overhead. Everything was too silent. Gracie pressed the circular *3* button, sending them into motion. Once they reached the third floor, he was surprised to see the first decorative item was the large marshal logo star on the wall.

Gracie opened the glass door and Cameron followed her wordlessly through the reception area to a closed door with a brass nameplate that read *Dallas Brafford. Supervisory Deputy US Marshal.* She rapped three times softly.

"Come in," a disembodied baritone voice answered from the other side.

"It'll be fine," she assured Cameron before grasping the handle and pushing it open.

A burly man with a thick beard sat behind a large wooden desk covered in papers.

Gracie took the chair closest to the wall and Cameron dropped onto the seat next to her. Bane settled between them, panting softly.

Cameron studied Dallas Brafford, surprised by the man's appearance. He wore a short-sleeved polo with the marshal logo in the corner and when he pushed back from his desk and walked around it, he saw Brafford was wearing cargo pants and combat boots, like Gracie. Cameron had expected a businessman in a black suit.

He perched on the edge of the desk and extended a hand to Cameron. "Nice to meet you in person. I'm Dallas Brafford."

Cameron shook his hand.

"It's my understanding you saved my agent's life," Brafford said, jerking a chin toward Gracie.

Cameron's face warmed. "I just didn't want Phillip to kill her." That sounded as lame aloud as it had in his mind, but the alternative was admitting to Gracie's boss that he'd almost lost the woman he'd fallen in love with.

"I owe you a debt of gratitude. And I pay my

obligations," Brafford assured him. He reached over and scratched Bane behind the ears. "Looking good, Bane." The dog's tail thumped in appreciation, lightening the mood slightly.

Brafford pushed to stand and returned to his seat. "We have details to work out regarding your transition, and as you're well aware, time is of the essence."

"We haven't found any other people besides Phillip and the missing Imogene, who might be connected to Cameron," Gracie explained.

Brafford passed Cameron a picture. "This was inside Phillip's jacket pocket." The photo showed Cameron with a big red *X* across his face. "It was taken by cell phone."

He studied the picture, instantly recognizing the back side of the ranch. Cameron's throat tightened with emotion.

"I also have an update regarding Imogene." Brafford withdrew a file and opened it. "Deputy marshals located evidence pinpointing the burial site for Imogene."

"Phillip killed her?" Cameron gasped.

"Yes." Brafford shook his head. "Still, without definite confirmation as to whether Phillip shared your identity with anyone else, I can't risk your life, Cameron."

"I fully expected you to say that." Cameron tried and failed to disguise the bitterness in his tone. He fidgeted nervously and shuffled forward to perch on the end of the seat. Unsure where to put his hands, he folded them on his lap, then changed his mind and flattened his palms on the armrest.

Gracie shot him a quizzical look.

"I'm a little nervous," Cameron said.

"After everything that's happened, I imagine you're on edge. I'm truly sorry for all that you've endured."

"Thank you," Cameron replied lamely.

"Based on what we know and our inability to interrogate Philip—" Brafford said.

Cameron cringed. They couldn't question a dead man. Thanks to him.

"—we're prepared to issue you a new identity and move you," Brafford concluded.

"What about my ranch?" Cameron asked.

"We'll handle the sale."

"Actually, sir." Cameron inhaled a fortifying breath. "I'd prefer Joel Iverson be given first option. He'll take good care of it."

"Absolutely," Brafford said. "You made Pronghorn Hills Guest Ranch into a fine business. I appreciate you wanting to see it continue to succeed."

"I hate to see it fall into a corporation's hands."

"Understandable," Brafford said, compassion filling the marshal's eyes.

"Ranching is natural to me," Cameron explained. "Wherever I'm sent next, I'd prefer that career."

"Hmm. I'll check," Brafford replied.

"I appreciate it very much, sir. Thank you for the consideration."

"Cameron, you carried the weight of what others

did to you. I recognize the unfairness of the situation, but understand from our perspective, without your help, Walter Quigley would have gotten away with murder. And who knows what other crimes Phillip committed that we have yet to uncover. Because of your bravery in coming forward, they were held accountable."

Cameron nodded, again at a loss for words.

"Maybe Walter taught his son his underhanded ways. I don't imagine he woke up one day and decided to become a criminal."

"Are you touting the nature-versus-nurture theory?" Cameron asked.

"Possibly. That's for folks with bigger brains than mine. What I can say is Phillip was the same age you were when his father was incarcerated. He had as much time with his dad as you did with yours. It seems to me, your parents raised a remarkable man. You've overcome adversities, and thrived in every situation WITSEC placed you. That says a lot about your character."

Humbled by the comment, Cameron looked down at his boots. "One of the few consistencies I had was Silas Rutherford as my handler. With his retirement, can you tell me anything about my new one?"

"His name is Ormand Engel. A retired and highly decorated navy SEAL. I had the honor of working with him a few years ago."

"And regardless where I'm sent, will Mr. Engel remain my handler?"

"Yes. I assure you that I will be there when the transition happens, and I have vetted Engel beyond my personal knowledge of him."

What else did Cameron have but to take Brafford at his word?

"I appreciate you meeting with me personally. I'll be in touch with details on your relocation and occupation." Brafford stood, dismissing them.

Cameron and Gracie rose, left the office and silently exited the building. They loaded into Gracie's patrol unit and started back for the DGTF headquarters.

By the time they'd reached the four-story brick DGTF headquarters in downtown Plains City, Cameron's mood had lifted.

"We're early," Gracie said. "Mind if we take a short walk?"

"Sure."

With Bane leashed beside her, they entered a grassy area on the right side of the structure, where picnic tables dotted the space. They strolled to a stone-and-flower cross, where a picture of a man and engraved plaque read *In Memoriam. Kenyon Graves.*

"Who was Kenyon Graves?" Cameron asked.

"The detective who was killed in the line of duty while investigating the gun traffickers for the task force," Gracie replied.

Cameron recalled her mentioning a little about the incident when they'd first talked.

"He had two small children who will never know

their dad," she said. "All for nothing. He didn't have to die."

Cameron's heart squeezed with compassion for the kids.

Gracie placed her hand on the plaque and closed her eyes. He stood quietly in reverence for the moment.

When she lifted her head and turned to face him, shimmering tears welled. Everything within Cameron wanted to pull her into his arms. He shoved his hands into his jeans pockets to stop himself.

"No children should have to deal with loss," Cameron said.

"Loss at any age is hard, but I agree," Gracie said.

"I always hate the phrase that 'children are resilient.' Just because they learn to cope doesn't mean they are resilient. I was eighteen and losing my parents made me an orphan. It was devastating." The confession erupted from his lips before Cameron had thought it through.

"I was twenty-five," Gracie replied. "And I still felt orphaned. You're right, it was horribly painful."

"I've never met anyone who understands me as you do," Cameron said. "Talking to you is easy. I don't feel like I'm burdening you with my story. It's more as if we're sharing our experiences."

"Exactly." Gracie wiped at her eyes. "Doesn't the Bible talk about how we learn to comfort one another with the same comfort we receive?"

"After all that's happened, how do you keep your

faith strong?" Cameron asked, not argumentatively, but in honest inquiry.

"Faith is the only thread holding me together. We cope with loss, heartbreak and horrible acts." She turned to look at the plaque again. "But God remains the same, regardless of my circumstances. That gives me hope. I know I'm never truly alone."

"I spent a lot of time being angry at God. Blaming Him for everything that happened and asking why He allowed it a hundred different ways," Cameron admitted. "I realize bad things happen, life is horribly unfair sometimes, but people like you, who reach out to make the world a better, safer, place… that gives me hope."

"I'm glad." She touched his hand. "Cam, God can handle your anger and your questions because He loves you. Just like a child to a parent."

"Yeah. My mom used to say that, too." Cameron nodded. "Truth?"

"Always."

"I'm tired of blaming Him. I want to have hope again."

They meandered lazily around the area, giving Bane time to sniff.

"Gracie." Cameron paused, facing her. "When I saw Phillip prepared to shoot you, I knew I'd do whatever it took to protect you. For the first time, my heart wasn't numb." *I am in love with you.* The words lingered on his lips, but he dared not say them. Another glance at the plaque and he reminded himself Gracie had an important job to do. She wasn't a WITSEC handler, just filling in as needed.

And with that insight, Cameron accepted once he had his new identity, Gracie Fitzpatrick would be gone forever from his life. He stepped back, distancing himself emotionally and physically. Thankful he'd not confessed his feelings, Cameron was determined to shut down any romantic notions. He'd helped her when it mattered most and that had to be enough for him.

Whatever future WITSEC chose for him would have to suffice without Gracie in his life.

THIRTEEN

Gracie sensed the subtle shift in Cameron's demeanor, preventing him from openly sharing whatever was on his mind. In an instant, an invisible emotional force field dropped between them. Her stubbornness kicked in, and she led him to a picnic bench. "After spending time with you on your ranch, I can appreciate you wanting to continue working on one. A life in the country away from chaos sounds like a wonderful place to raise a family." She bit her lip, wondering if she'd revealed too much.

Cameron stood a foot from her, maintaining distance. "Yeah." A sadness lingered in his reply. "You mentioned wanting a family someday. Would you continue working in law enforcement?"

"No, it wouldn't be easy, but I'd call it doing something different."

"You'd give up your career?"

"I'd make a change. I've heard it said people change their jobs up to four times in a lifetime." She exhaled. "Speaking of, I'm glad you spoke up and made the request to continue ranching."

"Me, too." Cameron's disposition softened slightly. "Even if Brafford isn't able to work out the specifics, at least it won't be because I didn't ask." He sat down on the table at a healthy and obvious distance. "Do you ever regret going into law enforcement?"

"Not in choosing the marshals," Gracie said. "However, if given the opportunity, I'd choose to have a life beyond my job." Did she dare open her heart and confess what had consumed her since their first meeting? Gracie studied him. Their time together was dwindling away. She had nothing to lose by telling him she'd fallen for him. If he didn't feel the same way, they'd go their separate ways, and she could lick her wounds alone. It was now or never.

"Is that bad?" Cameron asked, drawing her back to the conversation.

She blinked, replaying what they'd discussed before her mind took another route. Oh, right. Her career. "Dedication to the job is essential. Going in with less than full attention could get me, or my team, killed. But there must be a balance, too."

"Woman cannot live on job alone," he teased, and Gracie recognized the Bible reference about living on bread alone.

She smiled. "Exactly. My job provided the best distraction from my everyday life. It gave me other things to focus on, but I used it as a place to hide when I wanted to avoid dealing with hurt. After my parents and sister died, my work gave me reprieve from my emotions. Then, when Rod and I broke up it was the final straw in dealing with the loss and loneliness that overwhelmed me." She sighed. "The shake-up changed me. And the funny thing is, when I met you, Cam—"

At the use of his nickname, he lifted his eyes to meet hers.

"—I didn't know love would feel this way. I never felt for Rod the way that I feel for you. Even in such a short amount of time, we have a stronger connection than he and I ever did."

A long pregnant silence hung between them. Gracie's optimism started to fade at the conflicted expression on Cameron's face. Finally, he said, "I appreciate that, Gracie, and I echo your sentiments. You've had me reconsidering the possibility of a future with—" He didn't say *you*, but she saw it in his eyes. "But as you're fully aware, I'm being sent back into Witness Protection under a different identity. My life will never be my own."

"You don't have to go alone," she said.

He blinked. "What are you saying?"

"Cam, I've never felt this bold, but if I don't say this, I'll explode. I am in love with you. And as strange as that might sound, and as forward as it might be, we don't have the luxury of a lengthy dating relationship."

"You want a relationship with me?"

"Yes." Gracie smiled. "I'd walk away from my life in the marshals office today, if it meant having a future with you. I'm ready for the dreams I thought were dead. I want a family of my own."

"Whoa. Do you hear yourself?" Cameron stared at her and swallowed hard. "Gracie, I will forever live looking over my shoulder. Phillip found me once and flat admitted his dad had plans for my demise."

"I work in law enforcement. I'm always watchful for danger." Though she tried to infuse lightheartedness into her tone, she sensed Cameron's struggle and feared his rejection. "All I need to know is if you feel the same way for me?"

He pushed off the table. "Gracie, if I speak those words, I can never take them back." He turned. "Please excuse me, I need the restroom."

Hurt and confused, Gracie stood and escorted him to the building, entering the keypad code. "Down the hall to the right," she said.

Cameron hurried off without looking back.

Cameron burst through the men's restroom doors. His pulse raged in his ears and his stomach was tied in a hundred different knots. If he hadn't fled from Gracie's presence as fast as he did, he would've pulled her into his arms and confessed he'd fallen in love with her.

And he couldn't do that. His throat constricted. Hearing her say she was in love with him had filled his heart with a warmth he'd never known before. He'd desperately wanted to agree and share how he felt. Cameron needed to tell her how the thought of being away from her for one single day made him want to refuse WITSEC.

But Philip Quigley had found him and almost killed Cameron, Zach and Gracie. He wouldn't take that risk with her life. He'd already lost everyone he'd ever loved, and at one time, he believed he'd never recover from the pain. If he lost Gracie too… No.

That possibility had almost become a reality when Phillip nearly shot her.

He had no right to knowingly endanger Gracie, even if she signed on voluntarily for the risk. He'd bear the responsibility for her life if she joined him in WITSEC.

He paced the men's room, replaying their conversation.

Gracie mentioned she'd given more credence to others than to God for her value. Was he taking on the role of protector even though he had no right to? God had never left Cameron even when he'd tried walking away.

Could he trust God to protect Gracie? Had he also misplaced his trust and confidence, not in others, but in himself?

Gracie was a deputy US marshal. She was strong and smart, and a valiant warrior. She'd more than once proven she could handle herself in any situation. Gracie, by the very nature of her job, had already accepted the risks that came with facing danger. She'd chosen that lifestyle long before him. She was no damsel in distress. But more than that, Gracie's faith and values proved she trusted God with her life.

Cameron was running from her the way she'd run to her job. He didn't want to lose her, but he was willing to flee rather than face the wonderful possibility of loving her. Being without her felt like the worst punishment imaginable.

The voice in the back of his head continued to argue the point, and Cameron did his best to shove it aside. The bottom line was Gracie opted into situations where she could help people. If she joined him in Witness Protection, he'd be dragging her into his mess of a life, and it would cost her the career she loved.

Dragging…or inviting? Hadn't she asked?

The hurt that passed over her beautiful face when he'd practically run from her nearly ripped his heart in half. *Ugh.* He stared at his reflection in the bathroom mirror. "I am the biggest jerk."

He turned on the faucet and splashed cold water on his face, then took several paper towels to dry off. Again, staring at his reflection, he could no longer deny the truth. "You're afraid to ask her to marry you. You're afraid you'll fail her."

Cameron considered Gracie's words about faith and a scripture his mother often quoted bounced from the recesses of his mind. *Faith is believing what you don't see.*

It's taking that leap from the known to the unknown.

He'd spent twelve years alone.

Resolve consumed him. Whatever it cost, whatever the unknowns, he'd rather face them with her than spend another second without Gracie.

Defeated, Gracie and Bane returned to the yard. She walked to Kenyon's memorial, rereading the engraved words. She pondered his two young children, orphaned because of a heartless criminal with no regard for human life. They'd suffered the loss of their father and would never have a future with him.

But wasn't that true of all loss?

She replayed the conversation with Cameron. Until she'd said it aloud, she wasn't sure she could confess her willingness to leave the marshals. But she didn't regret a single word. Even though his reaction wasn't what she'd hoped for, she'd been honest with him and herself. With or without Cam, she was ready to pursue a new career path.

Again, her gaze flitted to the memorial. What about the commitment she'd made to the team to take down Kenyon Graves's killer? She owed them and Kenyon's children, didn't she?

Yet, she told Cameron she'd given up her own dreams to live purely for the job. She didn't want that to be her only legacy. Gracie had witnessed enough retirements to know once she left, they'd move on, and she'd have nothing left but a shadow box with her badge.

When Brafford mentioned moving Cameron, the breath had evaporated from her lungs. She couldn't imagine never seeing him again. But she wanted the best for him, even if it meant being without her.

Her mother's soft voice reminded Gracie that the only way to deal with tough situations was to pray and ask God for wisdom. Gracie bowed her head. "Lord, You know every detail of every life, the beginning and the end. I may never understand why bad things happen to good people or why awful people get away with the horrible acts that they do. Lord, I pray wisdom for what to do next. I feel so foolish." She'd hoped confessing her feelings to Cameron would have him doing the same. Instead, he'd rejected her. He'd literally run away from her. "If it's not me, Lord, please give Cameron someone special who will love him." The heartfelt prayer released Gracie, and yet they were the toughest words she'd ever uttered aloud.

If Cameron didn't have the same feelings for her, she still wanted him to experience true love. After all, what right did she have to expect him to embrace the idea of running off in the sunset with a woman he barely knew? Ugh. Had she really proposed that to him?

Gracie rubbed her temples, wanting to crawl under a rock. She couldn't offer to just date him. That's not how Witness Protection worked. And after her missteps with Rod, she'd not live with a man unless they were married. Cameron no doubt understood that, too.

Great. She'd essentially proposed to a man for the first time in her life and he ran away. "Nice, Gracie," she muttered. She hadn't been a great judge of character, based on her relationship with

Rod. But everything within her saw beauty in Cameron. He might not share her feelings, but Gracie was positive she wasn't wrong about him.

There was no turning back now. She'd expressed her heart and that in no way obligated Cameron to reciprocate. At least when they parted, he'd know how she felt about him.

When he finally returned, she'd let him off the hook. Maybe her time with the marshals wasn't finished yet. She'd work hard and do whatever necessary to help the team bring Kenyon's killer to justice and give his sweet children closure. Then pursue other options for herself.

Gracie bowed her head with one final prayer not to become bitter or angry about Cameron's rejection. He had a lot to deal with and she'd not ask more of him than he could handle. She cared too much for him to burden him that way.

Footsteps got Gracie's attention.

She reluctantly lifted her head to see Cameron standing a short distance away, hands shoved in his pockets, looking younger than his thirty years. "I didn't mean to interrupt."

"You didn't," she replied, "I was finished." She got to her feet, approaching him. "Cam, I apologize—"

"I love when you call me that," he interrupted. "I'll miss it when I'm given a new name."

Gracie blinked. "Beg your pardon?"

"I never liked being called Cameron, but when you call me Cam…" His voice trailed off and he shrugged. "I don't know. I just like it."

Gracie smiled. "My mom always said I had a way of nicknaming everything and everyone. I'm glad it didn't offend you."

"Not at all."

"I apologize if I made you feel uncomfortable or pressured by telling you what was on my mind. It wasn't my intention. I just figured it was now or never. And I wanted you to know how I felt, so you could make an informed decision. Whatever you chose." She swallowed hard and blinked. "Ugh. I'm rambling. Forgive me."

"There's nothing to forgive," Cameron replied, then walked closer and reached for her hand. "There's no Witness Protection dating program."

She smiled. "Precisely my thoughts."

"Can we sit?" He led her over to a picnic table. "I feel really vulnerable and weird now."

Great. She had made him feel uncomfortable and he didn't want to hurt her. "Hey, honest. No need to make excuses or try and protect my heart. I had no right to put you in that position."

Cameron's lip quirked. "Gracie, I value what you have to say, but you gotta give me a second to speak."

Gracie blinked, then giggled. "Right. Go ahead."

"As an adult, I have never not known a life without loss. I was eighteen years old when I lost my family. They were everything to me and I've never had anybody else to share my life, dreams or thoughts. I never felt comfortable doing that, anyway, and it wasn't safe even if I had found someone."

"I understand," she said, looking down at her boots and wishing that the moment would pass faster.

Cameron gently placed a finger under her chin and lifted her face to meet his. "But you changed everything. You made me realize all the things that I never had and had given up hope of ever wanting were still in my heart. I cannot imagine a life without you."

"Really?" Her heart thrummed faster, pulse racing in her ears. "But you said—"

"I know what I said," he interrupted. "Can I be blunt and horribly vulnerable with you?"

"Please do," she said. "I hate to be the only one feeling this way."

He laughed. "Gracie, I've never even had a serious relationship. How could I?" He shrugged. "I've never had a long-term girlfriend."

She'd not considered his lack of experience.

"I don't know how to act around you. I've forgotten how to be myself. I'm used to lying about who I am and trying to remember my pretend history. But you know everything. I have nothing left to hide from you."

Gracie remained silent.

"Being with you makes me feel safe emotionally. I can be honest, and blurt I've never had a girlfriend and still not feel like you're judging me."

"I wouldn't do that," she said.

Cameron looked down. "I've never had the experience of bringing a girl home to meet my parents."

Sadness for him filled Gracie.

"I wish you'd known them. My mother's laugh was contagious. Even if she was being silly, she'd have my dad and I in stitches."

Gracie smiled as Cameron shared.

"My dad was a jokester, big on playing practical jokes. But not mean ones," he clarified. "Just little things that made my mom and I smile. He was wonderful and taught me a lot." His expression sobered, the jovial mood fading. "I often wondered what it would be like to father my own kids. I'd become bitter, realizing that wouldn't happen for me. Not to mention, the one time I make an effort to try dating, and the woman becomes a fatal attraction."

Gracie chuckled. "Well, there is that." She paused. "I never considered how isolated your life was. I'm truly sad for all you missed with your parents. Adulthood with my folks was amazing." Her throat tightened with emotion. "I miss them every single day. And I miss my sister even more. You would've liked them, too, and I think, more importantly, they would've really liked you."

"You do?" Cameron tilted his head.

"Absolutely."

Cameron's gaze stayed fixed to hers. "Gracie, you said that you would be willing to give up your entire world for me. Do you understand the ramifications of what you're offering? You're a deputy US marshal. You'd have to surrender your entire identity, career and past."

She nodded, glancing at Bane and recalling their

work together. She'd loved being a handler. "Cam, without my career, I have no family to return to. And I can't work forever."

"Won't you miss the thrill of taking down criminals?"

"Probably. I'll end up developing my own true-crime podcast," she half teased.

"You'd succeed at anything you did."

Gracie studied Cameron. The strength of his jaw, his enrapturing blue eyes and his lips. "I'm ready for something more. I'm ready to share my life with you. I want to experience the joy of being a wife and a mother."

Cameron pulled her close, capturing her in a kiss that deepened with their combined dreams, hopes and the longing of a future together.

Gracie's knees weakened and she leaned into Cameron, allowing his strength to hold her up.

"Well, then." Cameron pulled away from her and kneeled on one knee.

Gracie's breath hitched. "Cam—"

"Gracie, would you marry me and join me in a bizarre adventure in Witness Protection?"

Tears blurred her vision, and she nodded unable to speak past her constricted throat. Finally, she squeaked, "Yes."

Cameron rose and pulled her into a hug. His kiss was tender, and Gracie melted under his embrace.

Her cell phone buzzed again, reminding her she needed to attend a task-force meeting being held upstairs. She reluctantly pulled away from Cam.

"I'll take you to a safe waiting area," she said, taking his hand and leading him into the building.

Gracie raced to the meeting, bursting into the room. Zach offered a quirked eyebrow as she settled into the closest open chair. Her face warmed with embarrassment at her tardiness and the news she'd have to share.

Detective West Cole, tech analyst Cheyenne Chen and Officer Jack Donadio were seated around the table. DGTF Leader Daniel Slater stood at the head of the room. FBI Agent Liam Barringer and Officers Lucy Lopez and Jenna Marrow joined via video conferencing.

"Now that everyone's here," Daniel said, gaining the room's attention. "Thank you all for joining in today. I have new information I wanted to share with you."

The in-person attendees flashed curious looks and leaned closer.

Daniel continued, "I received an anonymous tip from our John Doe trafficker that Petey Pawners's dead accomplice is none other than thirty-four-year-old Jared Olin from Keystone, South Dakota."

"That's my stomping grounds," Zach inserted. "I'll start asking around about him."

"Great." Daniel nodded. "Lucy, please join Zach in the interviews. Additionally, remember that anyone connected to Olin could be also involved in the trafficking ring, so every detail matters. Pay attention, ask lots of questions. Make sure each lead takes you to another. Criminals make mistakes. Let's find those."

Echoes of "Roger that" and "affirmative" filled the room.

"Zach, you have the best duty station," Cheyenne said, closing her laptop. "Keystone and Mount Rushmore are amazing. Not to mention all the wildlife."

"Yeah, it's a great place to live," he said, but his enthusiasm had withered. Gracie spotted the faraway look in his eye. No doubt, Zach was thinking about his wife, Eden, and the state of their marriage.

A twinge of guilt for the joy she felt around Cameron pricked at her. Maybe now wasn't the time to tell the team she was leaving. Yet, she didn't have the luxury of casually mentioning it. Daniel would need to replace her and once Brafford gave her the new Witness Protection identity documents, she'd have to leave. Gracie offered a silent prayer for Zach and Eden, hoping they would be able to work through whatever issues hurt them. She prayed for God to encourage him.

"Gracie, I believe you have an update for us as well?" Daniel said, gaining her attention.

Show time. "Um. Yes." She sat up straighter, sliding into marshal mode for confidence. "First, we confirmed Phillip Quigley was behind the attacks on Cameron Holmes. However, even with his demise, we cannot determine with finality whether Phillip revealed Cameron's identity to anyone else.

The marshals are giving Cameron a different identity and location effective ASAP."

"That's too bad," Cheyenne said.

"Yeah, after seeing his ranch, it'll be a huge blow for him to have to surrender that," Zach replied.

Gracie nodded. "It is, but Cameron's made peace with the change."

It was so hard to say goodbye to her team. She just needed a few minutes to collect herself.

Daniel continued, "Thanks, Gracie. On a personal note, I also have an update for you all." Again, with the team's full attention focused on him, he said, "I discovered little Joy and I are related on my father's side. As of right now, I don't have details and I'm still investigating her biological parents."

"I'll help," Cheyenne said, then quickly added, "If you need it."

"Thanks." Daniel offered a smile of affirmation. "I'd be grateful for any assistance. It's been more of a challenge than I'd anticipated." He addressed the group. "That being said, I appreciate your support in this. Joy is a sweet little girl and I want to ensure she has the best home possible. In order to do that, I have to know as much as I can about her."

"Totally understandable," Gracie replied.

The others chimed in their agreement.

"All right, team—" Daniel began.

"Actually," Gracie interrupted. "I also have an announcement." Her mouth went desert dry and her pulse raged in her ears. Why was she so nervous?

Gracie swiped her damp palms over her pant legs and shifted in her seat. Her heart was certain of the decision to leave the marshals and join Cameron, but telling the group was still difficult. She exhaled and said, "I have enjoyed working with you all. This team is incredible."

Immediately, downtrodden faces and frowns met her gaze.

Gracie pressed on. "However, I am pursuing the other side of Witness Protection."

Only Zach smiled, as he put the pieces together. The others appeared confused.

"During the course of our investigation. Cameron Holmes and I fell in love." Gracie lifted her hands in surrender. "Didn't mean for it to happen, but it did. As I explained earlier, since we're unsure whether his identity was compromised, he remains in danger. It's not possible for him to return to the ranch, so he'll be transferred. But he won't be going alone. I'll be joining Cameron…as his wife." The last word hung in the air and Gracie wondered if she'd spoken it.

A silence hovered in the room, and Gracie swallowed hard. Her gaze roved between her teammates, as she gauged their reactions. To her surprise, none seemed disapproving. She only saw kindness in their eyes.

"That's fabulous!" Cheyenne said, breaking the silence.

"Yes," Zach replied. "We're so happy for you."

"That's exciting," West said. "Love shows up

when it's ready to. Good for you in making the leap of faith." Gracie knew West and Tricia McCord had fallen in love during the time he was investigating the DGTF case.

"I think falling in love is one of the greatest things anybody could ever do," Jenna replied.

Humbled by their kindness, Gracie said, "I hate leaving you all, and I feel like I'm letting you down with Kenyon's case."

"Negative," Daniel replied. "There will always be cases for us to work. But you're entitled to have a life of your own. We wish you the very best."

"Hear! Hear!" the entire group declared.

Their approval eased Gracie's concerns, confirming she'd made the right decision. And she couldn't wait to start her life with Cameron.

EPILOGUE

Two days later...

Cameron stood beneath the flowered garland draped above the stable entrance, facing Gracie. She took his breath away in the simple white gown that wrapped her in elegance. Her dark hair hung in thick curls, framing her face.

Bane panted softly beside them, wearing a bow-tie collar.

His gaze roamed the small group present to witness their nuptials and ceremony. Since neither he nor Gracie had family, a few of her team members joined them.

"Ready?" Gracie's boss, Dallas Brafford, asked, taking his place between them. He'd been incredibly supportive of Gracie's decision to leave the marshals and marry Cameron—and he'd taken great care when it came to relocating them. For that, he'd always be grateful.

"Yes," Cameron said, hoping he didn't sound ridiculously eager.

He couldn't believe after today, he and Gracie

would be married. A month prior he'd assumed he'd live and die alone. Now, he had the most amazing woman in the world to spend his life with. There was still a chance he could be found, but he and Gracie would face everything that came at them together…as husband and wife.

"Welcome, everyone," Brafford said, initiating the ceremony.

With every word, Cameron's gaze remained fixed on Gracie. She offered a gentle smile, accentuating her beauty. A soft breeze blew her hair, causing the dark tendrils to dance around her shoulders. She had never looked more beautiful, and Cameron feared he was dreaming.

"Cameron and Gracie, repeat after me," Brafford said.

Cameron held Gracie's hands as they repeated their promise to love and honor one another, forsaking all others.

When they'd completed their vows, Brafford said, "Cameron, you may kiss your bride."

The words came faster than he'd anticipated them, but Cameron didn't waste a second. He leaned down, placing one hand to the small of Gracie's lower back, and pulled her closer. Cameron inhaled Gracie's sweet perfume, and captured her lips in a kiss that sealed their promise to one another and their dreams for a future together.

The group applauded, forcing them to part too soon.

"We have the rest of our lives to finish that kiss," Gracie whispered against his lips.

"May I introduce, Mr. and Mrs. Holmes," Brafford proclaimed, then whispered, "At least for today." He offered a wink and Cameron grinned. He and Gracie weren't allowed to share their new identities with anyone after the ceremony.

The group again applauded, and Bane barked happily.

Gracie faced him, her smile reaching her eyes. "I love you," she said.

"I love you, too."

The group moved to the tables set up on the grassy area and Cameron and Gracie celebrated with a small cake.

Before he knew it, Brafford approached having changed into his cargo pants and polo. "I'm sorry to interrupt this celebration, but we have to get on the road."

"Understood," Cameron said, flicking a glance at Gracie, who was mingling with her teammates.

As though sensing him, she met his gaze and nodded. With a few last hugs, she hurried to his side. "Ready?"

"Are you sure you want to do this? There's still time to back out," Cameron teased, praying she didn't take him up on the offer.

"Are you kidding? You're stuck with me for life." Gracie winked. "Marrying you is the best decision I ever made." She inched up on her tiptoes, wrapping her arms around his neck and kissing him again.

"I will never get tired of those," he admitted.

"Promise?"

"Promise."

"Good. Me, either."

With her hand in his, they loaded Bane and slid into the back seat of the blacked-out SUV with Brafford driving.

"I think he's excited to start this adventure," Gracie said. "Thank you again for letting me adopt him."

"Call it my wedding gift," Brafford replied.

She snuggled against Cameron until Brafford pulled up to the private Cessna plane on the small airport tarmac, waiting to take them to their new ranch in Texas.

Gracie looked down at the envelope containing their new identities. "I can't wait to start our life together."

Cameron drank in his wife with his eyes. "Then let's not waste a single second getting there."

* * * * *

Dear Reader,

I hope you're enjoying the entire Dakota K-9 Unit series. Thank you for joining Cameron, Gracie and K-9 Bane on their dangerous mission. I enjoyed writing this book for many reasons. Who doesn't love Deputy US Marshals, heroic Belgian Malinois dogs and the beauty of Badlands National Park? A fabulous story combination!

I have visited South Dakota a few times and I loved Badlands National Park. My family and I ventured there for a summer trip, and I found it to be an amazing place with incredible scenery. There's so much to see with the spires, rock formations and wildlife...all of it is truly awe-inspiring. The perfect setting for a suspense story! But it was also a powerful reminder to me of how majestic and amazing God is.

I love hearing from readers, so let's stay in touch. Join my newsletter, where you'll be the first to hear about my new releases, get behind-the-scenes exclusives on my books and more! Sign up at my website: www.shareestover.com.

Blessings to you,
Sharee Stover